The Maxwell Mystery

The Maxwell Mystery

By

Carolyn Wells

Enhanced Media
2017

The Maxwell Mystery by Carolyn Wells. First published in 1913. This edition published by Enhanced Media, 2017. All rights reserved.

Enhanced Media Publishing
Los Angeles, CA.

First Printing: 2017.

ISBN-13: 978-1548823283.

ISBN-10: 1548823287.

Contents

I: Concerning Opportunities 7

II: "Maxwell Chimneys" 12

III: The Belted Earl 19

IV: Saucy Mildred 24

V: The Tragedy 31

VI: "He Shot Me!" 37

VII: A Search for Clues 43

VIII: The Inquest 49

IX: Further Testimony 55

X: Mildred's Strange Story 60

XI: The Black Spangles 65

XII: An Interview With Milly 72

XIII: The Mysterious Missiles 79

XIV: In Pursuit of the Earl 85

XV: The Earl's Story 92

XVI: The Gray Motor-Car 99

XVII: Big Jack Judson 106

XVIII: A Pistol Shot 113

XIX: Red Ink Spots 121

XX: Irene Tells the Truth 125

XXI: Circumstantial Evidence 131

XXII: Fleming Stone's Discoveries 137

XXIII: The Confession 142

I: Concerning Opportunities

"PETER KING—Please—Peter King—Peter King!"

With a telegram on his tray, the bell-boy traversed the crowded hotel dining-room, chanting his monotonous refrain, until I managed to make him realize that I owned the above name, and persuaded him to hand over the message.

It was short, and extremely characteristic of the sender.

House party. Take afternoon train Saturday. Stay Tuesday.
I. G.
- PHILIP MAXWELL.

I was more than willing to take the designated train, and looked forward with satisfaction to a few days of pleasure. Philip had a decided genius for arranging parties of congenial people, and, moreover, the telegram assured me that at least one of my fellow guests would prove attractive.

For the letters "I. G." meant nothing more nor less than that Irene Gardiner would be there. Though I had met this young woman only twice, she already exerted a fascination over me such as I had never before experienced. As I had hoped, she too went down to Hamilton on the afternoon train, and the four hours' journey gave me an opportunity to cultivate her acquaintance more informally than at our previous meetings.

This pleased me, and yet when we were comfortably settled in our chairs, and rushing swiftly through the monotonous and uninteresting landscapes of central and southern New Jersey, I was conscious of a certain disappointment regarding my fair companion.

In the daylight, and on a railroad train, she lost the subtle charm which perhaps had been imparted by the glamour and artificial light of a ballroom; and she looked older and less ingenuous than I had thought her.

And yet she was a beautiful woman.

Her clear dark eyes were straightforward without being piercing; nor were they soulful or languishing, but capable of a direct gaze that was both perceptive and responsive. Her clear-cut mouth and chin betokened not only a strong will, but a strong character and a capable nature.

No, seen by daylight there was no glamour about Irene Gardiner, but the very lack of it, where I had expected to find it, interested me.

She was entirely at her ease as we pursued our journey, and with a ready, graceful tact adapted herself to all the exigencies of the situation. Perhaps it would be more nearly true of Irene Gardiner to say that she adapted situations to herself. Without seeming to dictate, she anticipated my wishes, and made just such suggestions as I wished to carry out. Within an hour of our leaving New York, I found myself enjoying a cigar in the smoker, and wondered how I had managed it. When I realized that I had come there at her advice and even insistence, I gave her immediate credit for tactful cleverness—woman's most admirable trait. Yet somehow I felt a certain chagrin. To be sure I did want a smoke, but I didn't want to be made to smoke;—and to obey the suggestion unconsciously at that!

There was no one in the smoker that I knew, and after I had finished my cigar, I began to feel a strong inclination to return to Miss Gardiner's society, and with a sudden intuition I felt sure that this was just the result she had intended to bring about, and that she had dismissed me in order that we might not both become bored by a long and uninterrupted tête-a-téte.

This very thought determined me not to go back; but such is the perversity of the human will, that the more I stayed away, the more I felt inclined to go. So half angry at myself I returned to my chair in the parlor-car, and was greeted by a bright smile of welcome.

"I've been reading a detective story," she said, as she turned down a leaf and closed the paper covered book she held. "I don't often affect that style of literature, but the train-boy seemed of the opinion that this book was the brightest gem of modern fiction, and that no self-respecting citizen could afford to let it go unread."

"Don't scorn detective fiction as a class," I begged. "It's one of my favorite lines of light reading. I have read that book, and though its literary style is open to criticism, it advances a strong and tenable theory of crime."

"I haven't finished the story," said Miss Gardiner, "but I suppose you mean the idea that innocence is only the absence of temptation."

"That is perhaps putting it a little too strongly, but I certainly think that often opportunity creates a sinner."

"It is not a new idea," said Miss Gardiner thoughtfully; "I believe Goethe said 'We are all capable of crime—even the best of us.' And while he would doubtless have admitted exceptions to his rule, he must have thought it applicable to the great majority."

"It's impossible to tell," I observed, "for though we often know when a man succumbs to temptation we cannot know how often he resists it."

"But we can know about ourselves," exclaimed Miss Gardiner with a sudden energy.

"Honestly, now, if the motive were sufficient and a perfect opportunity presented itself unsought, could you imagine yourself committing a great crime?"

"Oh, I have a vivid imagination," I replied gaily, "and it isn't the least trouble to imagine myself cracking a safe or kidnapping a king. But when it came to the point, I doubt if I'd do it after all. I'd be afraid of the consequences."

"Now you're flippant. But I'm very much in earnest. I really believe if the motive were strong enough, I mean if it were one of the elemental motives, like love, jealousy, or revenge, I could kill a human being without hesitation. Of course it would be in a moment of frenzy, and I would doubtless regret it afterward, and even wonder at my own deed. But the point I'm trying to make is only that, in proportion to the passions of which we are capable, we possess an equivalent capability of executing the natural consequences of those passions."

I looked at Miss Gardiner curiously. She certainly was in earnest, yet she gave me the impression of a theorist rather than one speaking from personal conviction. And, too, it shocked me. She couldn't mean it, and yet the positiveness of her speech and the earnestness of her look indicated sincerity. With her animated dark beauty she looked just then like Judith and Jael and Zenobia all in one. It was not at all difficult, at that moment, to imagine her giving way to an elemental emotion, but the thought was far from pleasant and I put it quickly away from me.

"Let us leave ourselves out of the question," I said, "and merely admit that crimes have been committed by persons innocent up to the moment when strong temptation and opportunity were present at the same time."

"You will not be serious," she retorted, "so we'll drop the subject. And now, unless you make yourself very entertaining, I'll return to my story book and leave you to your own devices."

"That would be a crime, and you would commit it because you see your opportunity," I replied, whereupon Miss Gardiner laughed gaily, and abandoned her discussion of serious theories. I must have proved sufficiently entertaining, for she did not reopen her novel, and we chatted pleasantly during the rest of the journey.

"Is it a large and a gay party we're travelling toward?" I asked, as we neared Hamilton.

"I don't really know," said Miss Gardiner; "Miss Maxwell invited me, and the only other guests she mentioned in her letter, beside yourself, were Mildred Leslie and the Whitings."

"You mean Mildred's sister Edith, and her husband?"

"Yes, you know Edith married Tom Whiting. He's a most delightful man and the Leslies are dear girls."

"I remember Edith as a beauty, but I haven't seen Mildred since she was a youngster."

"Prepare yourself for a surprise, then; she's grown up to be the most fascinating little witch you ever saw."

"At any rate, Philip thinks so," I said, smiling, and Miss Gardiner returned an understanding glance.

"Yes," she agreed, "Philip is perfectly daft about her, but I don't think Miss Maxwell is altogether pleased at that. She's awfully fond of Mildred, but I think she would rather Philip should choose a different type for a wife."

"But I doubt if Philip will ask his aunt's advice in such a matter."

"Indeed he won't; nor his uncle's either. Phil's a dear fellow, but those two old people have spoiled him by humoring him too much; and now they can't be surprised if he insists upon his own way."

"Do you approve the match?" I asked, rather pointedly.

"No; I can't. Milly is a perfect darling, but she would lead Philip a dance all his life. She's a born coquette and she can't help flirting with everybody."

"She may try it with me, if she likes," I said, nonchalantly, and Miss Gardiner responded, "Have no doubts of that! She's bound to do so. I only wish you would involve her, or let her involve you in so deep a flirtation that Philip would lose his interest."

"My dear Miss Gardiner, don't you know that that would be just the way to pique Philip's interest, and defeat your own very admirable intent?"

"I suppose it would," said Irene, with a little sigh, and then our train drew into the Hamilton station.

Philip met us at the train with his automobile.

"I say, but you're late!" he shouted. "We've been waiting twenty minutes." He led the way to his big touring car, as shinily spick-and-span as a steam yacht, and bundled us into it.

"You sit back, Peter," he directed, "with Mrs. Whiting and Miss Leslie, and I'll take Miss Gardiner with me. We'll run around the country a bit before we go home."

I hadn't seen Mildred Leslie for several years and I was all unprepared for the change which had transformed the shy schoolgirl into one of the most beautiful women I had ever seen. She was of the apple-blossom type, and her frivolous, dimpled face was adorably pink and white, with big pansy-blue eyes, and a saucy, curved mouth. A riotous fluff of golden hair escaped from her automobile-veil, and the first glance proved the girl to be a coquette to her fingertips.

Her sister, Mrs. Whiting, was totally unlike her. She was a solid, sensible little woman, whose sole occupation in life seemed to be a protracted futile attempt to keep Mildred in order.

I took my seat between these two ladies, feeling that, for the next few days at least, my lines had fallen in pleasant places.

"I do love a house party at the Maxwells," said Mildred, "because the party never stays in the house. There are so many lovely, outdoorsy things to do that if it weren't for meals we'd never see the inside of the beautiful old mansion."

"It is a beautiful house," said Mrs. Whiting. "I almost wish it would rain tomorrow so that we might stay in and enjoy it."

"Oh, Edith, not tomorrow!" cried Mildred; "we've too many things planned. Why, Mr. King, there's a different picnic arranged for every hour in the day, and you can pick out whichever ones you like best to go to."

"I've such faith in your taste," I replied, "that I'll just follow you, and go to the ones you attend."

"I'm going to send regrets to several of the picnics," announced Irene Gardiner, "and ramble around the house. I've never seen it, but I've often heard of its glories."

"We must stay indoors long enough to have some music," said Mrs. Whiting; "I want to hear Irene sing some of her old songs again."

"I cannot sing the old songs," Irene said, laughing; "but I know a lot of new ones."

"I'll stay home from any picnic to hear them," said Mildred promptly.

"I'll stay, too," said I, but though this sounded as if a compliment to Miss Gardiner's music, a flash of appreciation from Mildred's blue eyes proved to me that she read my intent.

II: "Maxwell Chimneys"

"OH, how stunning!" cried Irene Gardiner, for just then we whizzed up the driveway to the Maxwell house, and though perhaps not the word a purist would have chosen, "stunning" did seem to express the effect. The white pillars and porticoes of the mansion gleamed through the evergreen trees that dotted the broad lawn; the sunset in progress was of the spectacular variety, and a nearby lake reflected its gorgeous colorings.

Alexander Maxwell had chosen to call his beautiful home "Maxwell Chimneys," and the place was as picturesque and unusual as its name. It had chimneys of the reddest of red brick, and these stuck up all over the roof of the many-gabled house, and also ran up the sides and down the back, and nestled in corners, and even presented the novel spectacle of a fireplace right out on the broad front veranda.

Though Philip had laughed at this addition to the heating facilities of the mansion, it proved to be a great success, and on cool summer evenings the open fire lit up the atmosphere gaily and, incidentally, warmed a small portion of it. The truth was, Miss Maxwell did not herself like outdoor life; so, by filling her home with cozy fireplaces, she often enticed her guests indoors, which thoroughly pleased her hospitable soul. For the great house was always filled with guests, and one house-party followed close on the heels of another all summer long. "Maxwell Chimneys" occupied one of the most desirable locations in Fairmountain Park, and the views from its various windows and balconies were like a series of illuminated postcards. Or, at least, that was the remark made by seven out of every ten of the guests who visited there.

As we neared the veranda, a cheery voice shouted "Hello," and Tom Whiting ran down the steps to meet us. The big, good-natured chap was a general favorite, and I cordially returned his hearty greeting. Then the wide front door swung open, and the old doorway made a fitting frame for the gentle lady of the house who stood within it.

Miss Miranda Maxwell was Philip's aunt and, incidentally, was his devoted slave. She and her brother Alexander had lived in the old house for many years, beloved and respected by the townspeople of Hamilton, though deemed perhaps a shade too quiet and old-fogy for the rising generation.

But this was all changed when their nephew Philip came to live with them, and filled the house with young life and new interests. He had been there about three years now, and though the village gossips had concluded that he would never make the gentleman of the old school that his uncle was, yet he had won his own place in their regard, and his gay, sunny nature had gained many friends for him.

Phil was a good-looking chap of about twenty-three and had been an orphan since childhood. After his school and college days, his uncle had invited him to make his permanent home at "Maxwell Chimneys," and Philip had accepted the invitation. It was generally understood that he would eventually inherit the place, together with Alexander Maxwell's large fortune, and though not avaricious, Philip looked forward complacently to a life of ease and luxury. So far as social life went, he was practically master of Maxwell Chimneys; he invited guests whenever he chose, and entertained them elaborately. Though Mr. Maxwell joined but seldom in the young people's festivities, he paid the bills without a murmur, and smiled indulgently at his merry-hearted nephew.

I had known Philip all through our college days, and I had made long and frequent visits at Maxwell Chimneys, where the hours of quiet enjoyment were often varied by delightful impromptu entertainments, the product of Philip's ingenuity. I was a favorite with both the old people, and I fully returned their regard. Mr. Maxwell was a collector in a modest way, and I was always gratified when I could assist him in his quest or researches.

Miss Maxwell had such a kind, motherly heart that I think she was a friend to everybody, but she, too, seemed specially to like me, and so my visits to Hamilton were always pleasant occasions.

"How do you do, Peter? I'm very glad to see you," she said, so cordially, that the warm welcome of her tone made the commonplace salutation a heartfelt one.

"How do you do, Miss Miranda?" I responded, with equal cordiality. "I'm most happy to be here again. It is a long time since I've enjoyed your hospitality. Ah! here is Mr. Maxwell; how do you do, sir?"

I raised my voice to speak to my elderly host, for I remembered his deafness. He shook hands, and greeted me warmly, expressing his pleasure that I was with them once again. I counted this brother and sister among my best friends, and aside from their kindness and hospitality they represented the best type of our American people. Educated, cultured and refined, they imbued their home with an atmosphere of pleasantest good humor.

The house was luxurious, and their manner of living, though rather elaborate, was not formal and not uncomfortably conventional.

Miss Maxwell herself showed me to my room, and as she left me at the door, she gave a motherly little pat to my shoulder, saying: "Now, Peter, dear boy, Philip's man will look after you, but if everything isn't just to your liking let me know, won't you?"

"Sure he will, Aunt Miranda," broke in Philip's gay voice, as he passed us in the hall; "look alive, now, Peter, old boy, and tog yourself for dinner at once; and drop down to the terrace as soon as you're ready."

But after I was dressed, I stepped out onto the balcony through my own window, lured by the beauty of the scene before me. The distant hills were purple in the late twilight, and the crisp air of early autumn was pleasant after the warmth of the house. I stood at the balcony rail, and as I looked down I saw two people strolling along the terrace just beneath me. In the dusk, I was uncertain who they were, and then I heard Philip's clear, deep voice: "You're a rattle-brained, butterfly-minded and extremely conceited young person," he declared, "but I have the misfortune to love you as I love life itself; so, once more, Mildred, darling, won't you marry me?"

Mildred laughed. "Philip," she said, "I do believe that's the thousandth time you've asked me that question. Please don't do it again. My answer is—No."

"Milly," and Philip's voice took on a new tone, "I shall ask you that question just once more. Not now; and only once more. Remember, dear, only once. Come, let us go back to the house."

I felt no compunction at my involuntary eavesdropping, for these people were speaking in casual tones, and any one on the verandas might have overheard them. And, too, what they said was no secret. Miss Gardiner had told me that Philip wanted to marry Mildred, and I felt sure that the laughing reply she had given him was merely coquetry, and that he would again ask her the same question and get another answer.

I went downstairs and met the pair just entering the house, and then we went in to dinner. Later on, as was the custom at Maxwell Chimneys, we all gathered on the front veranda to watch the moon rise. Now, moonrise over Fairmountain was of the nature of a solemn function, and by no means to be lightly treated. The feminine members of the party, therefore, had selected their places with a view to their own picturesque effect in connection with the view and the men naturally fell into position near the women they most admired.

This, of course, meant that Philip Maxwell should establish himself in the near vicinity of Mildred Leslie. But the young man had learned by experience that Mildred's nature was possessed of a certain butterfly quality, that often caused her to hover about from one place to another, before settling on a final choice. And as he could not, with dignity, jump up and run about after her, he wisely paused, and stood carelessly leaning against a pillar, watching her as she fluttered about.

The young man had certainly shown no error in taste in admiring Mildred. She was without doubt the prettiest girl present, and prettier than any girl one would meet in many a long summer day. Her piquant, merry little face was always smiling, and her deep blue eyes seemed to be full of half-hidden sunshine. Her hair was just on the darker side of golden, and owing to a bewitching waviness seemed to look prettier every new way she arranged it. Mildred was not quite twenty, and had not outgrown a certain childish willfulness that was inherent in her nature. But though sometimes provokingly saucy, she was so winsomely attractive that her friends declared her adorable, in spite of the fact that she was a spoiled child. Philip's devotion to her was an open secret, and though there were others whose devotion was equally evident, the somewhat strong-willed young man had determined to win her, and of late had felt that he might consider his case hopeful.

In her dainty white evening gown, befrilled with fluffy laces, Mildred was a picture as she flitted about, from one group to another, the filmy blue scarf trailing around her, never in place, but always picturesque.

"Dear Miss Maxwell," she said, pausing a moment by her hostess' chair, "mayn't we have a picnic to Heatherwood, someday, soon?"

"Oh, do let us," chimed in Irene Gardiner, "a real old-fashioned picnic, with devilled eggs and lemon pie."

"My dear girls," replied Miss Maxwell, "you may have a picnic at Land's End if you choose, provided you don't ask me to go to it." For though Miss Miranda wanted young people about her, she didn't fancy running around much.

"Dear old Dearie," said Mildred, patting her shoulder, "she shall stay at home if she wants to, and toast her toes at her own fire-side, so she shall. Edith, you'll chaperon us, won't you?" she asked of the young matron of the party.

"In name only," said Mrs. Whiting, laughing; "but as to exercising any real authority over you rollicking creatures, I shouldn't like to promise it."

"Now, Mrs. Whiting," exclaimed Irene, "that's too bad! Milly, we all know, is difficult, but I'm as good as gold. At least, I have my good days; they're Tuesdays and Sundays this summer, and as tomorrow is Sunday you needn't worry at all about me."

"That's a lovely plan of yours," said Mildred, "to have days on which to be good. I wish I had one. I think one would be enough for me."

"You!" exclaimed Gilbert Crane, a neighbor who had strolled over; "you'd have to choose Tib's Eve, or the thirty-first of February."

"How delightfully rude you are," said Mildred, her dimples deepening, as she slowly drawled out the words at him; then, as if it were an afterthought —" I love rude men."

"It's nice of you to put it that way," he responded, "and as a reward I'll take you for a walk. Come on, we'll go and hunt up that moon. I don't believe it's ever going to rise over that mountain. Must have slipped a cog, or something."

"Thank you so much," said Mildred settling herself complacently in a rustic chair beside Miss Maxwell, "but I'm not going out this evening."

"Oh, yes, you are!" declared Crane in a gaily commanding tone, "just gather up that undecided blue wrap that seems to be detaching itself from your personality, and come along with me."

"Observe me go," said Mildred calmly, as she sat motionless in her big rattan easy chair. Gilbert Crane laughed, and sat down beside her, and began to chat in low tones, paying no attention to Philip's haughty look. Presently their attention was arrested by what Miss Maxwell was saying.

"Yes, he's coming tomorrow," declared that lady, with a note of triumph in her voice. She had been reading a telegram which a servant had just brought her, and as she folded it away, Mildred asked:

"Who is coming tomorrow?"

"Clarence, Earl of Clarendon," was the proud reply.

"Goodness! What a name! He ought to have it dramatized. But I suppose we can call him Clare or Clarry. Is he a real live earl, and what's he coming for?"

"Yes, he's real," said Miss Maxwell, in reply to the first question. "I was so afraid he wouldn't come, that I didn't tell you I had asked him. But he is coming, and all you girls must make yourselves particularly charming, and give him a good time. His people were perfectly lovely to us in England, so we must reciprocate. He'll be here in time for your picnic, Milly."

"He won't like me," said Mildred, pensively. "I'm too Stars and Stripesy to please an English earl. He'll succumb to Irene's statuesque charm and Vere de Verean repose of manner."

"Yes, of course, Clarence will think Irene the gem of this collection," agreed Edith Whiting; "but let's put up a brave fight, Milly. If we can't charm the belted gentleman, let's at least impress him with our free-born Americanism. We can attract his attention in some way, unless he's hunting an heiress."

"Why are earls always belted?" asked Mildred, drowning Miss Maxwell's protest at Edith's last words.

"They deserve to be belted for coming over here and bothering our girls," said Philip.

"I sha'n't bother with him," declared Mildred. "United States boys are good enough for me;" and she cast an approving glance at the good-looking young American men standing about.

"That's all very well," said Gilbert Crane, "and I hope you won't bother with his Earlship; but, I say, Milly, if you cast those big blue soup-plates of eyes of yours at him, I shouldn't like to answer for the consequences. You know English girls stare, they don't dart fascinating glances through a regular Niagara Falls of eyelashes; and I prophesy that his Belted Highness won't know where he's at, when you've smiled at him a few."

"Nonsense," said Mildred; "he won't give me a chance to look at him. Those English grandees are awfully stuck up, and they only come to quiz us and write us up. What does he look like, Miss Miranda? I suppose, as Lord Fauntleroy says, he doesn't wear his coronet all the time."

"I won't tell you anything more about him," rejoined Miss Maxwell, decidedly. "It isn't fair for you to know about him when he doesn't know anything about you."

"I think," said Tom Whiting, "I shall draw up a sort of descriptive catalogue of you girls, and nail it on the inside of his door. It will save him lots of trouble. Something like this, you know: Miss Irene Gardiner, raving beauty of the Burne-Jones type; classic features, amiable disposition, great tennis player and all-round athlete."

"There's no use going any further than Irene," interrupted Edith, with a disheartened sigh; "after that description, Clarence won't read any more."

"Wait and see," said her husband, laughingly.

"Next, we have Mrs. Whiting; a perfect blonde, of the peaches and cream variety. Sings like an angel and plays the mandolin to beat the band."

"That ought to charm any old earl," declared Crane; "now hit off Milly, though no mere words can do her justice."

"Ah, there's the rub!" exclaimed Tom. "If anyone can describe Mildred Leslie they're welcome to do it. I can't."

"I'll try," said Crane, "and if my descriptive powers give out, somebody else can take up the tale. To begin with, I should say Miss Mildred Leslie is a mischievous, roguish, saucy, adorable bit of humanity, who flirts with everybody within hailing distance—"

"I don't!" put in Milly, making a *moue*.

"You do," asserted Philip.

"Go on, Gilbert; a willful, perverse, spoiled child, who always has her own way -- "

"Because everybody is so good to her," interrupted Milly again.

"Because everybody loves her," said Miss Maxwell, looking affectionately at the young girl. At which Mildred kissed that lady's hand, and suddenly jumped up and ran away.

Later, when their hostess declared it was growing chilly, and they would go indoors and have some music, Philip came upon Milly and myself in a vine draped corner of the veranda.

"See here, Milly," he said, "you're not to let that foreign popinjay tie himself to your apron strings."

"Oh, do you suppose that's what he is coming over here for?" asked the girl, dropping her voice to an awestruck tone.

"If you weren't you, Milly, I should say you are a goose!" and Philip's tone actually sounded vexed. Mildred's manner became coldly dignified, but her eyes gleamed as she said, "Why, that's what I wanted to say to you."

At that Philip laughed genially. "Then let me beg you again not to let the Britisher tie himself up with any of your danglers."

"I certainly sha'n't ask him to," said Mildred carelessly, "but if he sees fit to tie himself, I can't help it. And you must admit, Phil, it would be a novel experience to have a real earl at my beck and call! Oh, I'd love to be proposed to by a nobleman! How do you suppose they do it, Philip?"

"You ought to know all there is to know about how men propose; you've been through it often enough."

"Yes, but it's almost always you, you know."

"I only wish that were true."

"Well, it is—almost," Mildred sighed. "But anyway, I like you better than most of the others; you're a lot nicer than Gilbert Crane, for instance."

"Well, I am glad you think so!" and Philip squared his shoulders with an unconscious air of superiority.

"You needn't act so conceited over it!" Mildred exclaimed. "Of course, you're big and handsome—and he's insignificant looking; but he can't help that, and you oughtn't to be vain."

Philip tried to look modest and self-depreciatory, but only succeeded in achieving a satisfied grin, whereat we all laughed.

"But you know," Mildred went on, "it isn't everything to be big and handsome and rich, as you are; and if I promised to marry you, I might afterward see someone I liked better."

"An earl, perhaps," said Philip, not noticing me, but looking at her steadily.

"Yes," said Mildred, returning his look with an unflinching gaze, "an earl, perhaps."

"Well," said Philip, giving her a curious look, "you might do worse."

"Indeed I might," she responded, a little curtly; "very much worse."

And, laughing a little at their foolish banter, I left them and went into the house.

III: The Belted Earl

CLARENCE, Earl of Clarendon, was arriving. Wherefore, the feminine guests at Maxwell Chimneys were peeping with careful discretion through curtains and window blinds, in their impatience to comment upon the appearance of the distinguished visitor.

But from their vantage ground they could see only a big, heavy-coated figure emerging from a motor-car, followed by a quantity of foreign-looking luggage.

"He's gone to his rooms," announced Milly, after a skirmishing peep into the hall, "and of course we won't see him until dinner time. Come on, Irene, let's go and put on our very bestest frocks. I wish I had a tiara or a coronet! Do you think I'd better wear feathers in my hair or just a wreath of roses?"

"I'm sure I don't know about earls," I put in, "but I'm sure, Miss Leslie, that most men prefer natural flowers to those fanciful confections that you young ladies sometimes perch on your heads."

"You tell us, Mr. Maxwell," said Irene Gardiner, as our host entered the room, "do you suppose earls prefer made-up hair ornaments or natural flowers?"

"Bless my soul! I'm sure I don't know," declared the bewildered old gentleman; "I never was an earl!"

"You ought to be," said Mildred, smiling at him; "your manners are courtly enough to grace any,—any—what do earls grace, anyway?"

"Well, as one will grace our dinner table pretty soon, it would be wise for you girls to run away and get ready to do your part of the gracing," said Miss Maxwell, smiling at pretty Milly, who was in her most roguish mood.

"I simply can't dress, Miss Miranda, until I decide between my silver filigree headdress and a wreath of pink roses."

"Nor I," said Edith; "I believe I'll wear a single rosebud."

"Yes, do," said Mildred; "do wear the simple little blossom, dear; it will make you look younger!"

As Edith was only two years older than her sister this could not be called an unkind sarcasm.

"Baby-face!" she retorted; "nothing could make you look younger, unless, perhaps, you carry a Teddy Bear in your arm."

"I've a notion to do just that!" said Mildred, laughing.

"I must shock that English prig, somehow."

"How do you know he's a prig?"

"All Englishmen are. I've never met any, but I'm sure they're snippy and critical, and not a bit like our own brave lads. I've lost interest in him anyhow. You may have him, Irene, if you want to."

"That's all very well, now, but as soon as you see him, you'll appropriate him."

"No, I won't, honest; I hereby make over to you whatever interest I may have had in the noble Earl of Clarendon, and promise not to interfere with your game, if you choose to add his very likely bald scalp to your other trophies of the chase."

"Oh, pshaw, that won't do a scrap of good if you even talk to him or look at him at all," said Irene, putting on a rueful look. "Just as Mr. Crane said, if you sweep your eyelashes round once, he'll be done for."

"All right," said Mildred; "then, furthermore, I promise not to talk or converse with the above mentioned Clarence beyond the ordinary civilities of the house; never to smile at him voluntarily and never to wave my eyelashes at him across the table. "And now," she rattled on, "I know I'll be late for dinner!" and then she ran away to her own room.

Presumably, she took great pains with her toilette, for it happened that she was the latest to enter the drawing-room. She had elected to wear a gown of palest blue organdy, which, though of simple effect, was in reality a marvelous confection, born of art and science.

Her hair was massed in a curly top-knot, secured by shining combs, and on her soft fair neck rested a string of wax beads, which she chose to call "The Leslie Pearls." Her cheeks were a little flushed with the exertion of her hasty dressing, and fear of tardiness lent her an apologetic air, half timid and half-cajoling, as she crossed the room to her hostess.

Miss Maxwell stood near the fireplace and smiled indulgently at the pretty dismay of her young guest. Mildred smiled, too, and then, raising her eyes, suddenly discovered that at Miss Maxwell's side stood six feet two of man, with the broadest shoulders she had ever seen!

"Oh," she almost gasped; "I thought…" and then she seemed to realize that a formal introduction was being made. She dropped a slight and very dainty curtsey, and as she was about to raise her eyes to the face which she naturally assumed surmounted this column of humanity, she remembered she had promised not to wave her eyelashes at him. Convulsed with the ridiculousness of the situation, she stammered a greeting which meant nothing, and resolutely turned her face away.

"What's the matter, Mildred; are you ill?" said Miss Maxwell solicitously.

"Oh, no, indeed," said Mildred, raising her blue eyes to meet the elder lady's glance, and just giving the Earl a three-quarter view of her really wonderful lashes.

"No—I—I, that is, I was afraid I would be late for dinner, you know."

"Nonsense, child; don't be foolish. Talk to Lord Clarence for a few minutes, before we go to the dining-room."

So Mildred dutifully talked, but, in a moment dinner was announced, and it fell to her lot to be escorted to the dining-room by my humble self.

"What's the matter?" I asked after we were seated at the dinner table. "Why did you turn down his Noble Nibs so soon? You scarcely spoke to him."

"Too English for me," said Mildred briefly, not wishing to discuss his lordship. "He's a handsome chap," I went on. "And he's a good, all-round fellow, too. I've been talking with him, and he's broad-minded and fair, with a keen sense of humor. Go in and win, Milly; I'll give you my blessing."

"No, thank you," said Mildred, turning her eyes resolutely away from the stranger. "Columbia is the 'Gem of the Ocean,' for me."

"Why don't you announce your engagement to Philip, and have done with it?" I said audaciously.

"One reason is, that I'm not engaged to him," said Mildred calmly.

"But you will be. He has every chance in the world."

"That's where you're wrong. There's only one chance in the world that I shall marry Philip Maxwell." She smiled as she remembered Philip's emphatic assurance that he should ask her once more only. "But I'm not going to marry anybody for years yet. Let's talk about something more interesting. Look at Phil, now! He's devotedly reciting poetry to Irene."

"Oho, that's your more interesting topic, is it? But, wait, the noble Britisher is making good. Just listen to that yarn he's telling. He's a ripping good story-teller." And Mildred, listening, was forced to agree.

On the terrace, after dinner, the party broke up into small groups of two or three, and Mildred, quite unintentionally, found herself talking to Lord Clarendon, or rather he was talking to her.

"Don't run away," he said, as she tried to edge off toward another group; "stay and talk to me."

"I can't talk to you," she said, stammering a little, "because—because—" and as he smiled at her, she continued, in sheer desperation, "because— because I don't know what to call you!"

"Don't you know my name?"

"Yes; but I don't know whether to address you as 'my lord' or 'your lordship.'"

She knew she was talking nonsense, but she was honestly trying to get away, and so said anything at random.

The Earl stood looking down at her, with his half-mocking smile.

"Either would succeed in attracting my attention, if I heard you; but why not call me Clarence?"

"It's a stunning name," said Mildred, "but I couldn't use it so soon. Indeed I never can."

With a sudden determination she turned abruptly and walked away, leaving him standing there.

"By Jove!" said his lordship to me as he looked after her; "I can't make her out at all; but she's a dear little enigma."

The evening wore away, and it was quite late when Mildred and I, again together for a moment, saw someone coming near. Then a kind voice over her shoulder said, "Is it possible that this little lady's afraid of me?

There was a laughing note in the voice, an amused, yet self-assured tone that seemed joyously confident and contradictory to the words.

I wondered what reply she would make, for the terrace in the moonlight was a dangerous place. Acting on a sudden impulse, whether courage or cowardice I didn't know, she whispered in a broken voice, "yes, I am afraid of you," and turned swiftly and suddenly away from him.

Philip was never very far away from Mildred's side, and though he was glad to notice her apparent lack of interest in the Earl, he was at a loss to understand her persistent rejection of the nobleman's advances.

"What's the matter with the Belted One, Milly?" he asked; "I'm sure I don't want you to churn with him, but why treat him with such desperate scorn?"

"I don't scorn him, but he doesn't interest me," said Mildred, a little impatiently, for she was beginning to be tired of her own game.

But Philip was not entirely unversed in the whims and ways of the Eternal Feminine, and he responded, "Oho! piqued, are you?"

"Indeed I'm not, and, pray, why should I be?"

"Oh, for many reasons. Perhaps because Clarence is so devoted to Irene. She'd look well wearing a coronet, wouldn't she? It would suit her tall stateliness a lot better than it would your petite effects."

"Don't talk any more about that horrid Earl. I'm tired of the thought of him."

"That's your attitude toward everything," said I.

"Oh, no, it isn't," she responded saucily.

"I never get tired of myself, and I'm not yet tired of you."

"Don't think of him, then," said Philip. "I'm truly glad, if you don't like him. But you're overdoing it so it made me a bit suspicious. You see, I know your tricks and your manners!"

"Am I very bad, Philip?" said Mildred, a little wistfully.

"You are indeed. You're a heartless little witch, and you'd not only flirt with a wooden Indian, but you'd know just the best way to go about it."

"Thank you for the subtle compliment. And yet—with all my faults, you?"

"Of course I do, and always shall! Does it please you to know it?"

"Not especially," said Mildred, her mocking eyes smiling gaily into Philip's handsome, earnest face. "And I sha'n't talk to you any more now, for you seem to have only two subjects of conversation—yourself and the Earl of Clarendon. And I don't care a straw for either."

Philip only smiled, for though Mildred's words sounded indifferent, the glance that reached him from beneath the long lashes belied the words, and, I am sure, strengthened his conviction that the butterfly heart was really his.

I left the pair then, and strolled away in the direction of Irene Gardiner.

IV: Saucy Mildred

"I'M so glad we're going to have a dance tonight," said Edith Whiting at luncheon next day.

"Oh, so am I," declared Mildred, "I'd rather dance than eat; and we haven't had a real party dance since we've been here."

"Give me four two-steps, won't you, Miss Leslie?" said I.

"Why don't you ask for eight steps; can't you multiply? Indeed I won't give you four two-steps, Mr. King."

"Oh, I so hoped you would!" I responded, in mock dejection.

"Why, how can you expect it?" she exclaimed.

"There'll be a lot of strange men here from all the country round, and I'm going to give them all my dances. I can dance any day with you men who are staying in the house."

"Do you mean that, Miss Leslie?" exclaimed Clarendon, in such apparent consternation that everybody laughed.

"On second thoughts, I'll give you one apiece, all round," said Mildred gaily.

Philip sat next to her at the table. "You'll give me more than that," he said in a low tone, "or else you needn't give me any."

"Very well," said Mildred airily, "you needn't have any. Lord Clarendon, if you care for two dances tonight, I have an extra one that has just been returned with thanks, which you may have."

"I accept it gladly, fair lady, but don't let it be one of your American two-steps, for I have not yet mastered their intricacies."

"They shall be any ones you choose," said Mildred, with a glance at the Earl, that was deliberately intended to delight him and to anger Philip, and succeeded perfectly in both cases.

"Mildred," said Tom Whiting, under his breath, as they left the table, "you are playing with fire."

"Perhaps I wish to get burnt," she retorted saucily, and ran laughing away.

That afternoon Philip and I chanced to find ourselves alone for a time. I was glad, for I hadn't had an opportunity to talk much with him.

We sat in a shady corner of the veranda and he looked moody and glum. Finally he threw his cigar away, and said, frankly, "What would you do with her, Peter?"

"Do you want me to answer you seriously," I said, "or flippantly?"

"Seriously, please."

"Then I think you'll have to teach her a lesson. You let her go too far, Philip; and you may find, when you try to curb her, you can't do it."

"I know I can't, King; she's reached that point already."

"Then begin as soon as possible. Tell her that she must either be engaged to you or not. And if she is engaged to you, she must stop flirting with the Earl."

"Good Heavens, Peter! it isn't the Earl that bothers me. It's someone quite different."

"Who?" I asked in astonishment, but just then we were interrupted, and I had no answer to my question. But it bothered me for a time; and I couldn't help wondering if by any possibility Philip could be jealous of me! It seemed absurd, for though of course I admired Milly Leslie, as everybody did, yet I wouldn't for the world have intruded upon Philip's rights. I could get no opportunity to speak to Philip again on the matter until that evening after dinner. The ladies had all gone away to dress for the dance, and Philip and I chose to stroll and smoke in the rose garden. But again my intention came to nought, for Earl Clarence joined us. Philip seemed in better spirits than in the afternoon, and he chaffed the Earl gaily, in an unusually merry mood.

It was after dark, but by the faint light of a moon which had not yet risen, we saw what seemed almost like a fairy being coming toward us. It was Mildred, and she was wrapped in a voluminous cloak of pale blue, beneath which showed a pair of dainty white dancing slippers.

"Oh," she exclaimed, drawing back as she recognized us, "I thought you were the gardener!"

"To which one of us did you pay that compliment?" inquired Philip, laughing.

"Oh, I won't be partial, I thought you were all gardeners," said Mildred drawing her cloak around her and seeming about to leave us,—though I felt sure she had no such intention, and was coquetting as usual.

"Do you want a gardener?" said I; "won't I do for one?"

"Well," and Mildred hesitated, "I was just dressing for the dance you know, and I found I must have,—simply must have some of those tiny yellow roses, that grow over there. I would have sent the maid for them, but I know she wouldn't select the very tiniest ones, and those are the ones I must have. So I thought I'd just run down and get them myself,—I never dreamed I'd meet anybody!"

Though the big blue eyes looked babyishly innocent above the closely held blue wrap, I felt a secret conviction that those same eyes had seen the group of men in the rose garden, and did not mistake us for a group of gardeners.

"I knew everybody was dressing for the dance," she went on, "so I thought I couldn't possibly meet anybody."

She pouted a little, as if we were to blame for interfering with her plan.

"It doesn't matter that you have met us, dear," said Philip, gently; "I'll cut some roses for you,—which ones do you want?"

Milly was a tease, there was no doubt about it. She smiled at Philip, and then turning deliberately to the Earl, said, "You're nearest to the yellow rose tree,—won't you cut me some, please?"

Philip spoke no word, but stood for a moment looking at the girl he loved. Then, in a tense, unnatural voice, he said, "Clarendon, will you look after Miss Leslie?" and, turning on his heel, walked rapidly away.

"Milly," said the Earl, eagerly stepping toward her. It was the first time he had ever addressed her so, but Mildred had no intention of precipitating matters in this unconventional situation, and, too, she was troubled at the remembrance of Phil's disapproving glance.

"Lord Clarendon," she said coldly, "will you be so very kind as to pick me a few yellow roses, and let me hasten back to the house?"

"There is plenty of time," he said quietly; "please give me a few moments."

"No," said Mildred, stamping her foot impatiently, "I wish to return at once."

"Very well," said Clarendon gently, "I will not detain you. Will you have this spray?"

He selected a charming cluster of roses, and taking his penknife from his pocket cut them for her, and stood trimming off the thorns.

"I wish I might have given you flowers to wear this evening," he said.

His manner was gentle and deferential, and I was sure Mildred felt perhaps she had been too brusque, as she said kindly, "I wish so, too; but how could you have bought any flowers way off here in the country?"

"I could have sent to town for them, or gone myself for them."

"But I oughtn't to accept real hothouse flowers from you –"

"Why not? Because it would mean a special favor on your part? But that is just what I want it to mean, dear little girl –"

"Oh, Lord Clarendon, please don't! Please give me my flowers and let me go."

"Will you consider them a gift from me, as I can't get any others now? And will you let them mean –"

"Oh no, they don't mean anything—not anything at all—yet."

He had taken her hands and placed the spray of roses between them, and still held the two little hands, roses and all, close clasped in his own.

Her long cloak, released, fell away, and the vision in the pale silken robe seemed to the noble Englishman quite the most beautiful thing he had ever seen. He caught his breath, as he looked at the baby face, with its troubled, beseeching eyes.

"Please let me go, Lord Clarendon—please!"

Then she gently disengaged her hands from his, and gathering up the folds of her blue cloak, prepared to run away.

But he detained her a moment. "Miss Leslie," he said, and his choking voice betrayed his passion, "I won't keep you now—but tonight you will give me an opportunity, won't you, to tell you –"

"Tonight, my lord, you are to have one dance with me, you know."

"One? You promised me two!"

"Oh, I never keep dance promises. I'm not at all sure I shall give you one."

"But I'm sure you will, you tantalizing baby! Now which shall be the first one that I may call mine?"

"Choose for yourself, my lord," said Mildred, in her most demure way.

"Seven is a lucky number, may I have number seven?"

"Yes, I'll save that for you," and, with a laughing glance over her shoulder, she ran away.

"What a little witch she is, to be sure, eh?" and Earl Clarence gave a short laugh.

"I beg your pardon if I offend," I said, a little stiffly; "but I think you,—that is we,—ought to remember that she is pledged to Philip."

"Ah, I did not know it was announced."

"Nor is it, officially. But in this country, we accept such a situation, without words,—if we are friendly with the people concerned."

"Indeed!" was the cool response; "but the men of my country have their own code of honor, and it is not to be impugned."

This was a fine opening for a quarrel, but as I had no intention of indulging in a dispute with our titled visitor, I said only, "I have no criticism to make of the English code of honor,—I'm sure!" and turning on my heel, I left his lordship among the yellow roses.

Soon after, standing in the lower hall, I watched Mildred Leslie come dancing down the stairs. She wore a short dancing gown of palest yellow chiffon, and in her shining curls nestled the tiny yellow roses.

It was an unusual color for a pronounced blonde to wear, but it suited her dainty beauty, and she looked like a spring daffodil.

Of course she was immediately surrounded by would-be partners, but Philip Maxwell was not among them.

"Sulky," said naughty Mildred, as I asked her where he was. "Well, it will do him good to worry a little."

As was usually the case, pretty Mildred was the belle of the ball.

She halved most of her dances, and changed her mind so frequently about her partners that she soon tore up her program, declaring it bothered her, and she should accept invitations only as each dance began.

She finished the sixth dance with me, and as we sauntered about after the music ceased, we met Philip apparently looking for her.

"The next dance is ours," he said looking at her in an unsmiling way.

"Indeed it isn't!" declared Mildred, who had by no means forgotten to whom she had promised the seventh dance.

"It is," said Philip sternly, "come!"

"Better go," I whispered in Mildred's ear; "he's in an awful huff!"

Meekly she allowed herself to be led away, and Philip took her out on the veranda.

"Now," he said, as they passed out of hearing, "with whom are you going to dance this next dance, with me or with that confounded foreigner?"

"With him, Philip," said Mildred, very quietly.

"I promised it to him before the party began."

I was thoroughly angry at the little coquette, and I turned away and strolled idly through the rooms. I did not feel like dancing, for the moment; and seeing Miss Maxwell, sitting alone in a corner of the drawing-room, I went and sat by her for a few moments' chat.

She seemed preoccupied, and after some perfunctory answers to my trivial remarks, she said:

"Peter"—she always called me by my first name, and somehow her soft, sweet voice gave the ugly word a pleasant sound—"there is something wrong with Philip. I can't imagine what it is, but for a week or more he has been so different. It began all at once.

"One day last week he came to luncheon looking so harassed and worried that my heart ached for him. I said nothing about it—we are not confidential as a family, you know—I only tried to be especially gentle and tender toward him. But he didn't get over it. He spoke sharply to his uncle, he failed to show his usual deferential courtesy to me, and he behaved altogether like a man stunned and bewildered by some sudden misfortune.

"I talked to his uncle about it when we were alone, and he, too, had noticed it, but could not account for it in any way. He though perhaps it might be money difficulties of some sort, and he offered to increase Philip's allowance. But Philip refused to accept an increase, and said he had no debts and plenty of spending money. So we are at our wits' end to understand it."

"Could it have anything to do with Miss Leslie?" I asked.

"I think so," replied Miss Miranda, looking about to make sure we were not overheard. "He is very much in love with her, and I think she cares for him, but she is such a coquettish little rogue that one cannot be sure of her. Besides, this trouble of Philip's began before he planned this house party, and before he thought of inviting Miss Leslie and her sister down here."

"Does he talk frankly to you about Mildred?"

"Oh, yes, he hopes to win her—indeed, he says he feels confident of succeeding. But I think he tries to persuade himself that he will succeed, while really she is breaking his heart over her flirtation with Gilbert Crane."

"Gilbert Crane!" I exclaimed, greatly surprised.

"Why, I thought she was flirting so desperately with the Earl."

"Nonsense! Mildred is just teasing Philip with him. When she flirts so openly, there is no danger. But she conceals her liking for Gilbert Crane. He's here tonight, and I'm sure I don't know what will happen."

"But Gilbert Crane! why he's a friend of Philip's."

"Yes, our fellow townsman, and one of Philip's best friends."

"But he can't hold a candle to Philip."

"I know it. Philip is rich, or will be, and Philip is handsome and talented, while Gilbert is none of these. But somehow he has a queer sort of fascination over Mildred, and she is certainly very gracious to him."

"Philip and Gilbert are as good friends as ever, aren't they?"

"Yes, I think so, lately. At least they were until lately. But Mildred's evident preference for Gilbert's society has wounded Philip, and though he treats Gilbert as kindly as ever, I've seen him look at him as if he wondered how he could play such an unfriendly part."

"You think, then, to put it plainly, that Gilbert is trying to win Mildred away from Philip?"

"I do, and I think Philip is as much hurt by Gilbert's treachery as by Mildred's fickleness. But I cannot think that it is this affair that worried Philip so last week. For then, Mildred hadn't come, and Gilbert was right here all the time, and he and Philip were inseparable. No, it's something else, and I can't imagine what."

"Phil seems about as usual to me," I said.

"Yes, he is much brighter since you young people came. More like his old self. But when he's alone, even now, he drops into an attitude of absolute despair. I've seen him, and it is something very dreadful that has come to my boy. Oh, Peter, can't you find out what it is, and then I'm sure we can help him."

I assured Miss Miranda that I would try in every possible way to do all I could to help, but I felt convinced that no one could help Philip at the present time, except Mildred Leslie herself.

Then Mr. Maxwell came in and joined us, and the tenor of our conversation changed.

I should have been glad to talk with him about Philip, but owing to his deafness I couldn't carry on such a conversation in the drawing-room.

But notwithstanding his affliction, Mr. Maxwell had a fine ear for music, and greatly enjoyed it. A piano, violin and harp furnished the music on this occasion, and as it was of exceedingly good quality, Mr. Maxwell sat and listened, tapping his foot gently in time with the rhythm. I saw him glance at Philip several times, and, if the boy was smiling, the old gentleman's anxiety seemed relieved, but if Phil was over-quiet or sober-looking, Mr. Maxwell sighed and glanced away again.

The drawing-room was the front room on the left, as one entered the great hall that ran through the center of the house. Back of it was the billiard room; back of that, Mr. Maxwell's study and behind that a well-filled conservatory.

On the right of the wide hall, the front room was the music-room; behind it was the dining-room, and back of that a short cross hall and a butler's pantry,—the kitchen being still farther back.

The large library was on the second floor, and was in many ways the most attractive room in the house. There were bedrooms on both the second and third floors, so that Maxwell Chimneys was well adapted for generous hospitality.

A broad veranda ran all around three sides of the house both on the ground floor and second story, and on it, from most of the rooms, opened long French windows.

After watching the dancers for a while Miss Miranda urged that I join them, and though I would have quite willingly remained with her, I did as she bade me.

"And, Miss Miranda," I said, as I left her, "don't worry about Philip's affairs. I hope—I'm sure you exaggerate to yourself his despondency, and I can't help thinking that soon matters will be brighter for him."

V: The Tragedy

I WAS fortunate in finding Miss Gardiner free to give me a dance, and in a moment we were circling the polished floor. She said little or nothing during the dance, and when it was over I took her for a stroll on the upper balcony, where, standing at the front railing we looked out on the beautiful country spread before us in the moonlight.

Irene Gardiner puzzled while she attracted me. I never could feel quite sure whether or not she was as frank as she seemed. Perhaps it was only the natural effect of her dark, almost Oriental beauty, but she somehow seemed capable of diplomacy or intrigue. Tonight, however, she was simply charming, and whether assumed or not, her attitude was sincere and confidential.

We traversed the three long sides of the house on the upper balcony and then, turning, retraced our steps. Frequently we met or passed other couples or groups of young people, and exchanged merry, bantering words.

At last Irene paused at the southeast end of the balcony, and we sat down on a wicker settee.

"Mr. King," she said, almost abruptly, "don't you think it's a shame, the way Mildred treats Mr. Maxwell?"

I was surprised at the question, but had no intention of committing myself to this mystifying young woman.

"Who can criticize the ways of such an enchanting fairy as Miss Leslie?" I replied lightly.

"Do you think her so fascinating?"

The question was wistful and very earnestly asked.

"She is both beautiful and charming, and she has completely bewitched Philip," I said.

"Yet she does not really care for him," cried Irene, passionately. "She adores Gilbert Crane, but she leads Philip on, and is breaking his noble, splendid heart, merely for her own amusement."

My eyes were opened.

"Oho, my lady," I thought to myself. "You are in love with the handsome Philip. Sits the wind in that quarter?" But I only said, "Gilbert Crane! do you really think so? Why I thought she was lavishing all her favors on our titled guest."

"Oh, he's only an incident. Milly sees that it teases Philip for her to flirt with the Earl, and she does so openly. But her liking for Mr. Crane is another matter. You men are so blind! can't you see that just because she doesn't flirt openly with Gilbert Crane, it proves that she's really interested in him?"

"She is only a child after all," I said, "and we must forgive her a great deal."

"On account of her youth and beauty!" said Miss Gardiner, in a tone that was positively bitter; "that's always the way! A baby face and golden hair and big blue eyes will excuse any amount of fickleness and treachery and deceit!"

"Those are strong words, Miss Gardiner," I said, amazed at her unkindness; "are you sure they are deserved by our little friend?"

"Yes; I know Mildred Leslie as she is! You men only know her as she chooses to appear to you!"

"I don't think I can agree with you, Miss Gardiner. If Mildred Leslie were of a deeper nature, I might think you are right. But she is as open as the day; a superficial, butterfly sort of girl, who cares only for the pleasure of the passing moment. I mean no disparagement, but I think that the light-heartedness of her nature is her best defense against your charges. I think she cares for Phil. And truly, in her heart. Who could help preferring that splendid fellow to young Crane?"

"I know it seems so," went on Irene, "but she does like Mr. Crane better. She told me so herself, only today. She said Philip is egotistical and purse-proud, and that Mr. Crane has a true poet soul."

"Perhaps she didn't mean her confidences for me, Miss Gardiner," I said a little stiffly, for I was of no mind to discuss these things.

"I don't care," cried Irene, her eyes blazing, "I'm telling you because I want you to know how matters really stand, and then I want you to warn Mr. Maxwell against such a fickle, shallow little thing as Mildred is."

"I can't consent to do that," I answered. "Philip is old enough to know what he is about. If Miss Leslie prefers Gilbert Crane, Phil will certainly find it out for himself, and soon. But I think he will convince her that she has only a passing fancy for Crane, and that he himself is really her destined fate."

I tried to speak gaily, for I did not wish to take the subject seriously. But in a low, tense voice Irene exclaimed:

"It shall never be! Philip Maxwell shall not throw himself away on a heartless little coquette who doesn't know how to value him! Since you refuse to help me, I will take matters into my own hands!"

I was amazed at her intensity of speech, but still trying to treat it all lightly, I said:

"That is your privilege, fair lady. Come, let us return to the dancing-room,—sha'n't we?"

"You go down, please, Mr. King," she said, and her voice was quieter. "Leave me here for a little, and I will rejoin you soon." As she seemed to be very much in earnest, I did her bidding, and sauntering around, I entered the house by the long French window into the front hall. As I passed through the hall, I met Miss Miranda just going to her own room.

"Leaving us?" I inquired, smiling at her.

"Yes," she said. "I am very weary tonight, and I have excused myself. Mrs. Whiting will look after you young folks, and I am sure she will ably represent me."

She looked not only tired, but worried, and I felt sure Miss Leslie's behavior was grieving her dear old heart.

"Don't worry, dear lady," I said, earnestly; "you know we must allow a certain latitude to frivolous, butterfly-minded little girls."

"Yes, I know it," and she smiled, slightly; "And I hope there is a true womanly heart under that mischievous nature."

"I'm sure there is,—and I'm sure it is devoted to our Philip. Don't take it too seriously; remember that Philip is not a weak sort of a man, and he is able to control his own affairs."

"But he is simply wax in Mildred's hands; she can do anything she likes with him. She can send him into the seventh heaven of joy or into the depths of despair by her smile or frown."

"I know it; but that has been lovely woman's privilege through all the world's history. We can't expect our Phil to escape the common fate. So cheer up, and let us hope that he will yet capture the pretty little rogue, and that they will live happy ever after."

"Thank you, Peter; you have cheered me up, as you always do; and I shall sleep better for your words of hope. Good night."

"Good night," I said gently, "and I trust you will rise tomorrow morning refreshed and happy."

"I hope so," she said. "Good night, Peter."

As I turned to go downstairs, I heard voices in the library, which I realized were those of Philip and Miss Leslie.

With no intention of eavesdropping, I couldn't help hearing him say: "Don't trifle with me tonight, Mildred; I am desperate." The tone, more than the words, struck a chill to my heart, and I hastened downstairs lest I should hear more of a conversation not meant for me. There were groups of merry people in the music room and in the drawing-room, but somehow I didn't feel like joining them, and I wandered back through the long hall, and looked in at the open door of Mr. Maxwell's study. This attractively furnished room could have been called a "den" by a younger man, but my host was conservative in his language, and adhered to old-fashioned customs.

I well knew it was his habit to devote an hour or two after dinner to his evening paper, which, naturally, never reached Maxwell Chimneys until late.

The household always refrained from intrusion on him at this time, and so, when I saw him intently studying the market reports, I turned away.

But he had seen me, and laying down his paper, he said cordially:

"Come in, my boy, come in and smoke a pipe with me, if you are tired of your young and somewhat noisy contemporaries."

"No," said I, going into the room, "not now, Mr. Maxwell. You finish your paper, and later, I'll drop in for a smoke. I'd very much like to have a talk with you."

"About Philip?" he asked, looking at me with a concerned air.

"Yes," I said, "but don't be apprehensive. Indeed, I think we may have cause to congratulate the boy before the evening is over. He and Miss Leslie are even now in the library, and I hope that they will arrive at a happy understanding."

"Good, Mr. King, good," said the old man in his kindly, pleasant way. "Let us hope for the best, and I trust it will all come out right."

"I'm sure it will," said I, and was about to go on, when he detained me a moment longer.

"What about that decorated Britisher?" he asked, looking at me intently.

"Oh, I'm told he isn't in the running," I replied, lightly; for, as Mr. Maxwell was deaf, I didn't care to discuss this matter in tones loud enough to be heard in other rooms.

"I dare say,—I dare say," Mr. Maxwell replied, but the blank look on his face made me think he hadn't heard me clearly. However, I went on through the study, and, lifting the portiére, passed into the billiard-room.

Here I found Gilbert Crane, alone, and sitting with his face buried in his hands in an attitude of deepest dejection.

I suddenly realized that, as I was obliged to speak to Mr. Maxwell in a loud, clear voice, Mr. Crane must necessarily have heard what I said.

He looked up as I entered, and his face showed bitter despair.

He said nothing, however, and as I had nothing in particular to say to him, I went on through the drawing-room, across the main hall and into the music-room.

Pretty Edith Whiting was dancing with a Mr. Hunt, whom I knew, and as I passed Tom Whiting, I praised his wife's grace. His kindly, good-natured face lighted up. "She is a beautiful dancer," he said, "try to get a turn with her, King."

"I will," I responded, and went on. I soon found a partner, and later, another, so that two or three dances passed before I had a chance to ask Edith Whiting.

But I finally did so, and with a pretty gesture she laid her hand on my arm and we whirled away.

It chanced that we were just opposite the door into the hall, when suddenly, Gilbert Crane appeared in the doorway. His face was white with terror and wild with fright, and he cried:

"Dr. Sheldon, Philip and Mildred have shot each other! Come up to the library. Quick!"

Although Dr. Sheldon was quick in his response to Gilbert Crane's summons, I was quicker, and, dashing upstairs, I reached the library door first, with Edith and Tom Whiting close behind me. Of course Gilbert's statement that they had shot each other was manifestly improbable, and was doubtless the irresponsible speech of frenzy.

My first glance at the tragedy showed me Philip stretched on the floor, apparently dead, and Mildred fallen in a heap, a few feet away.

I did not touch them, but I saw she had a pistol grasped in her right hand.

In a moment Dr. Sheldon and several others came hastening in. I had expected to see the whole crowd, but as I learned afterward, Lord Clarence, with rare good judgment and presence of mind, had insisted on most of the guests remaining downstairs until more particulars of the accident were learned.

Dr. Sheldon gave a quick look at Philip, flung open his clothing, placed his hand on his heart, and after a moment, said gently:

"He is dead."

Then he turned to Mildred, and stooping, took her unconscious form in his arms.

"She is not," he said eagerly. "Telephone for my assistant, Dr. Burton, to come at once and bring my instruments. I think we can yet save her life. Tell him to fly. Tell him what has happened, but don't delay him."

Dr. Sheldon, who was acting as rapidly as he talked, took the weapon from Mildred's hand and laid it on the table.

"Let no one touch that," he ordered, "and let no one touch Philip Maxwell's body. Send for the coroner at once. Mr. Crane, will you keep guard in this room? And, Mr. King, will you dismiss the guests, and inform Mr. Maxwell and his sister what has happened? Mr. and Mrs. Whiting will assist me with Miss Leslie."

Tom Whiting and the doctor bore Mildred to her room, and I, not at all liking the part assigned to me, went toward Miss Maxwell's door. But I suddenly thought of Irene Gardiner, and resolved to tell her first, thinking she could break the news to the dear old lady with a better grace than I could.

I stepped out on the front balcony, wondering if I would find her around the corner where I had left her, but to my surprise she was seated near the front window, and was weeping violently.

"Irene," I said, as I touched her shoulder,

"Miss Gardiner, do you know what has happened?"

"What?" she said, still shaking with convulsive sobs.

I told her, and her piercing shriek brought Miss Maxwell to her door.

"What is it?" she cried, as she flung open the door.

"What is the matter?"

Suddenly Miss Gardiner grew calm, and with a return to her own tactful manner, she took the old lady in her arms, and told her the sad news. Miss Maxwell's face turned white with grief and shock; she tottered, but she did not faint. Then her loyal heart prompted her to cry out:

"My brother! Does he know? Has he been told?"

"No," I said, "but I will tell him."

"Do," she said, "you know and love him."

Then, supported by Irene, she returned to her room. I hurried downstairs, and found Mr. Maxwell still alone and undisturbed in his study. It was the hardest task I had ever had to do in my life. The old man laid down his paper, stretched his arms, and said:

"Well, have you come for our smoke?"

"No, Mr. Maxwell," I said, "I am the bearer of sad news. Philip has been hurt."

"Eh?" he said, not quite hearing my words.

"Philip has been hurt," I repeated, "shot."

"Shot!" and the old man's face grew ashy pale, as he leaned back in his chair.

I had heard hints of heart disease, and I was thoroughly frightened. But just then Dr. Burton came in, and I begged him to take a look at Mr. Maxwell, even before he went upstairs to Mildred Leslie.

Dr. Burton gave the old gentleman a stimulant of some sort, and I resumed my awful errand. He was very quiet, seemingly stunned by the news, and after a few moments, his sister came into the room. I believe I never was so glad to see anyone in my life, and feeling now that they were better alone, I left them.

VI: "He Shot Me!"

I WENT next to the music-room, where Lord Clarence was dismissing the guests who, less than a half-hour before, had been so hilarious.

The Earl acted like a splendid fellow, and his cool head and capable management proved to be just what was needed for the sorry situation.

In a short time nearly all the guests had gone. Gilbert Crane remained, and Mr. Hunt, who was a sort of society detective, asked to be allowed to stay.

The coroner arrived just then, and learning in a few words the facts of the case, he advised Hunt to stay, for a time, at least. Miss Lathrop, a trained nurse, who had been sent for by Dr. Sheldon, also came, and she was taken at once to Mildred's apartment.

"Mysterious case," said the coroner, after a long look at the room and its contents. "Might be an attempt at double suicide, or suicide and murder."

"Or double murder," said Mr. Hunt.

The coroner gave him a quick glance. "We must work on evidence," he said, "not imagination."

"What evidences do you see?" asked Gilbert Crane.

"Very little, I confess," replied the coroner, who was a frank, straightforward sort of a man, and whose name, as I afterward learned, was Billings.

"But," he went on, "when a gentleman is found dead, and a wounded lady nearby, with a pistol in her hand, it doesn't require an unusual intellect to deduce that she probably shot him. Unless, as I said, it is a double suicide, and he shot himself first, and then she shot herself."

"Is Philip's wound one that could have been self-inflicted?" I asked.

"Without a doubt," replied Mr. Billings.

"He is shot directly through the heart, and that could have been done by himself or another."

"But of course we shall have medical evidence as to that."

"How about the powder marks?" asked the quiet voice of Mr. Hunt, who was already examining the room and taking notes.

"It is difficult to judge," answered Mr. Billings.

"The shot went through both coat and waistcoat, and while the powder marks would seem to prove that the shot was fired from a distance of three or four feet, yet I cannot say so positively."

I felt a certain relief at this, for while it was bad enough to think of poor Philip shooting himself, somehow it was worse to imagine Mildred shooting him.

Soon Dr. Burton came into the library. He talked with Mr. Hunt and Mr. Billings, and then said:

"As soon as you have completed all necessary investigations, Dr. Sheldon requests that the body shall be removed to Mr. Philip Maxwell's room and laid upon the bed, in order that it may seem less shocking to his aunt and uncle."

I liked this young doctor. He had Dr. Sheldon's clean-cut, assured ways, but he spoke and moved with rather more grace and gentleness. Dr. Sheldon had been a guest at the dance, which was fortunate, as it may have been the means of saving Mildred's life. But Dr. Burton looked as if he were not at all inclined toward gayeties. Serious, grave, he gave Dr. Sheldon's message, and then turned away, knowing he could do nothing more.

The coroner agreed to his suggestions, and later, I saw Mr. Maxwell and Miss Miranda go together to the room that had always been Philip's. As I look back upon that night now, it seems to me like a horrible dream—so many people coming and going, the servants beside themselves with grief and fright, and the dreadful facts themselves so mysterious and so difficult to realize.

It seemed impossible that Philip could be dead—merry, light-hearted Phil, who, except for the last week or so, had always been so gay and joyous. And Mildred Leslie's life hung in the balance. Dr. Burton's news of her had been this: she had been shot in the right shoulder, and the wound was dangerous but not necessarily fatal. Partially paralyzed by the shot, or perhaps only fainting from fright, she had fallen to the floor, and struck her temple as she fell, presumably against the corner of the table near which she stood. It was this blow which had made her unconscious, and which had left its mark in a huge, swollen discoloration on her fair brow.

She had as yet uttered no word, for she had been placed as soon as possible under the influence of ether, while the doctors probed for the bullet. It had been successfully extracted, and was now in Dr. Sheldon's possession.

Dr. Burton thought that Miss Leslie would soon regain consciousness, but deemed it exceedingly unwise to question her, or excite her in any way for some time to come. Indeed, he said he was sure Dr. Sheldon would allow no one to see her for several days except the nurse, and possibly her sister.

At last Mr. Maxwell and Miss Miranda were persuaded to retire, and the rest of us were advised to do so. But Gilbert Crane announced his intention of staying at the house all night.

He said some one should be in general charge, and as Philip's best friend he considered he had the right to assume such a position. He established himself in Mr. Maxwell's study, and told the servants and the doctors to call on him in any emergency. Seeing that Mr. Hunt sat down there too, with the evident intention of discussing the affair, I delayed my retiring and joined them. Lord Clarence looked in, and seemed to hesitate to intrude.

"Come in," I said; "as one of the house guests you surely have a right."

He came in, and almost immediately after, Mrs. Whiting and Irene came, and we went over and over the mysterious details.

"What were Mr. Philip Maxwell's sentiments toward Miss Leslie?" inquired the detective.

No one seemed inclined to reply, and as I thought it my duty to shed all the light possible on the case, I said: "I have good reason to believe that, at or about the time of his death, Mr. Maxwell was asking Miss Leslie to marry him."

"Did she favor his suit?" pursued Mr. Hunt.

"No," broke in Irene, "she did not. She told me so only this morning."

"But that would be no reason for her shooting him and then shooting herself," wailed Edith Whiting.

"Oh, I am sure Mildred never did it. Or, at least, not intentionally. I've reasoned it all out, and I think he must have been showing her his pistol, or explaining it to her, and it went off accidentally, and then, in her grief and fright, she turned the weapon on herself."

"Was it Philip's pistol?" asked Irene.

"Yes," said the detective, "that is, it had P. M. engraved on the handle."

"Oh, it was Phil's pistol," said Gilbert Crane.

"I know it well. And he always keeps it in the top drawer of that big table-desk they were standing by."

"How do you know they were standing by it?"

This question came from the Earl, who, though he had not spoken before, had been intently listening, and who now spoke in a curt, sharp voice, almost as if he were making an accusation.

"Because," said Gilbert quietly, "there were no chairs near the desk. They both fell near the desk. Philip could not have walked a step after that shot through his heart, and Mildred must have been standing near the desk to fall and hit her head on it. Am I clear?"

"Perfectly," said the Englishman, but his voice sounded ironical.

"Mildred never shot Philip intentionally," reiterated Mrs. Whiting. "She is a rattle-pated girl—a coquette, I admit—and she was not in love with Philip Maxwell; but truly she was no more capable of a murderous thought or instinct than I am. You know that, don't you, Irene?"

Irene Gardiner gave me one quick glance, and like a flash I remembered our conversation in the train about opportunity creating a criminal.

Could it be that pretty Mildred, holding a pistol in her hand, and alone with an unwelcome suitor could—no, I could no more believe it than Edith, and I flashed a look of amazed disapproval at Irene.

But she was already speaking.

"I'm sure Mildred didn't shoot Philip at all, Edith," she said. "I think he shot himself and she tried to wrest the pistol from him, and in doing so wounded herself."

This explanation struck us all as so plausible that we gladly accepted it—all of us except Gilbert Crane—and wondered we hadn't thought of it before.

Gilbert said slowly: "There could have been no struggle after that shot entered Philip's heart. If he shot himself, and Miss Leslie then took the pistol from him, it was after he had ceased to breathe."

"Was death, then, absolutely instantaneous?" I asked.

"Yes," said Mr. Hunt, "both doctors are sure of that."

Just here Tom Whiting came downstairs and joined us in the study. His face wore a peculiar expression. One of awe and perplexity, yet tinged with a certain relief.

"I think you ought to know," he said, "that Mildred is coming out of the ether's influence, and has spoken several times, but only to repeat the same thing over and over. She continually cries:

" 'He shot me. Oh, to think he should shoot me!' I tell you this in justice to my wife's sister."

"I knew Mildred didn't do it!" cried Edith, almost fainting in her husband's arms. "I don't care how black the evidence looked against her, I knew she never did it."

The next morning it was a sad party that gathered around the Maxwell breakfast table. After we were seated, the nurse, Miss Lathrop, glided in and took her place among us. It may have been prejudice, but I took an instant dislike to the woman from the way she glided in. Many trained nurses show a sense of their own importance, indeed, it seems to be a part of their uniform. But aside from this, Miss Lathrop gave an impression of knowing far more about the whole affair than any of the rest of us. It was by no means what she said that carried this impression, but rather, what she didn't say.

If one of us made an observation or expressed an opinion, she turned suddenly to the speaker, gave him a sharp look, and then dropped her eyes again, but with a little superior smile hovering round her thin lips.

It exasperated me beyond endurance, though I had no real reason to resent her attitude. In response to the queries we put to her, her definite news of Mildred was not encouraging. "She will have brain fever," announced Miss Lathrop; "Doctor Sheldon fears it, but I am sure of it. I have had great experience with patients of her temperament, and I know it cannot be averted."

She shut her lips together, giving the impression that since she so willed it, Mildred should have brain fever in spite of anybody.

"Has she talked at all?" asked Miss Maxwell.

"She has said nothing," replied Miss Lathrop, "except to repeat over and over again: 'Oh, to think that he should shoot me!' in surprised and agonized tones."

Probably from her enjoyment of a dramatic sensation, Miss Lathrop's voice and expression were almost theatrical, and though this jarred on all of us, it was especially harrowing for Miss Maxwell and her brother, who of course were the ones most deeply affected by Philip's death.

Poor old Mr. Maxwell was crushed, and unless someone spoke directly to him, paid little heed to anything that was said.

Miss Miranda, on the other hand, tried to forget herself and her troubles in caring for her guests.

It was pathetic to see her efforts to be cheerful and unselfish, and she seemed to me like a lovely saint ministering to unworthy mortals.

As Mr. Hunt had remained over night, he was at breakfast with us. It seemed a strange coincidence that he should have been present the night before, for surely he would be of help in unravelling the mystery.

While not a professional detective, he had proved successful in many difficult cases in which he had chosen to interest himself.

"I can't help thinking," Mr. Hunt observed, "that when Miss Leslie is rational again, what she tells us may throw a new light on the matter."

"I quite agree with you, Mr. Hunt," said Miss Lathrop, in her cold, concise way; "I have reason to think that Miss Leslie will yet make further revelations. And I'm sure we are very fortunate in having an able detective right here in the house."

Miss Lathrop flashed a glance at Hunt, which obviously implied she knew more than she cared to tell, and then, with her odious little smile, calmly proceeded to extract the seeds from her grapes.

Mr. Maxwell looked up with a pained face. Miss Lathrop's speech had seemed to rouse him almost to indignation.

"It is no case for a detective," he said, with a severity of manner I had never noticed in him before. "If, as Miss Leslie asserts, my poor boy shot her, that is all that is necessary for us to know about the affair. As to motive, my nephew has been seriously troubled of late, and doubtless his worry so disturbed his mind that he was irresponsible for his act. At any rate, I choose to consider him so."

"I'm sure we all agree to that," said Lord Clarence, in his kind voice; "not one of us can believe for a moment, that Philip Maxwell would commit such a deed, if he were sane at the time."

Miss Lathrop gave the Earl the benefit of one of her mysterious glances, and though she said no word, she clearly did not agree with him.

To my secret gratification, his lordship caught her up. "Have you definite reasons for not agreeing, Miss Lathrop?" he said.

Miss Lathrop was taken by surprise.

She colored slightly, and then pursing her mouth, said primly; "Professional ethics will not allow me to say."

"Professional ethics are out of place at this moment," said Mr. Maxwell, sternly. "If you know anything, Miss Lathrop, that will cast any light on this subject, it is your duty to tell us at once."

"I know nothing," Miss Lathrop said, shortly, and I, for one, believed she spoke truly.

VII: A Search for Clues

AFTER breakfast when Mr. Hunt started to go home, I accompanied him to the gate. Lord Clarence was also with us, and we both urged him not to go.

"I think it better that I should," Hunt responded; "Mr. Maxwell objects to seeing a detective about, and I can't blame the poor old man."

"I suppose it is a natural feeling," said Lord Clarence; "and, too, if Philip Maxwell did the shooting in a moment of temporary insanity, then, as Mr. Maxwell says, there is no occasion for detective work. But do you think that is the true explanation of the matter?"

"It is a possibility," I said, "though it's a new theory to me. But Philip was very much upset, indeed, deeply troubled for some unknown cause; and I, for one, do not think that cause was connected with Miss Leslie."

"Then why did he shoot her?" demanded Hunt.

"He didn't, intentionally. But if his mind was unbalanced, who can hold him responsible for his deed?"

"That's true," said Hunt. "Well, I suppose it will be all cleared up at the inquest. But since the perpetrator of this murder is not alive, it will doubtless be a mere matter of form."

"Where will it be held?" I inquired.

"Right here in the house, probably. Today or tomorrow, I should think; as the funeral will be on Thursday, and they can't bury him without a permit."

I shuddered at the dreadfulness of it all. Hitherto I had thought an ordinary death and burial sad enough, but how much worse with these attendant circumstances.

"Queer, nobody heard the shots," went on Mr. Hunt.

"Did nobody hear them?" I exclaimed. "I hadn't thought of that at all."

"And, yet your questions and opinions in the matter seem to imply a detective bent," said he, glancing at me a bit quizzically.

"I do take a great interest in detective work," I replied, "but I feel like Mr. Maxwell in this case. I see no occasion to detect anything beyond what we already know. It seems mysterious, I admit, but we know that one or both of the two victims did the shooting, and truly, to me, it doesn't much matter which."

"It does to me," said Gilbert Crane, who had joined us as we stood by the gate, and had heard my last remark.

"Well," said Mr. Hunt, with what seemed to me like a brutal cheerfulness, "if Miss Leslie gets well, we'll know all about it; and if she doesn't, we'll never know any more than we do now."

"If she fired either ball, she did it accidentally," declared Crane.

"Didn't you hear the shots either?" asked the Earl, turning on him suddenly.

"No," said Gilbert, "and I can't find anyone who did hear them."

"But you were first on the scene?"

"Yes, so far as I know."

"How did you happen to go up to the library just then?" asked Hunt.

"I didn't start for the library," said Gilbert slowly. "I was feeling pretty blue and forlorn, and the gay music jarred on me, so I thought I'd go home. I went upstairs for my banjo, which I had left on the upper front balcony in the afternoon."

"Was there any one on the balcony?" said Hunt, casually.

"I didn't see anybody," said Crane, "though I think I heard voices around the corner. But I didn't notice them; you know the house was full of people."

"I can't understand," pursued the Earl, thoughtfully, "why nobody heard the shots."

"Oh, I don't think that's so strange," returned Crane. "Mr. Maxwell is quite deaf, and Miss Maxwell is slightly so. And as for the young people, with the music and dancing, they wouldn't be apt to hear them."

"And you came directly downstairs after coming in from the balcony?" went on Hunt.

"As I reached the top of the stairs, I couldn't help looking toward the library, and as I heard no sounds, though I had been told Philip and Mildred were in there, I glanced in, I suppose from sheer curiosity."

"Who told you they were in there?"

"I did," said I, "or rather, I told Mr. Maxwell, in Mr. Crane's hearing. I saw them there when I went downstairs. That was, I should think, about half an hour before Mr. Crane gave the alarm."

"Can either of you fix the time of these occurrences?" said Mr. Hunt. He was very polite, even deferential in his manner, and I saw no harm in accommodating him.

"I can tell you only this," I said. "After I passed the library, where I both heard and saw Philip and Miss Leslie, I went on downstairs and looked into Mr. Maxwell's study.

"He asked me to sit down. I did not do so; but after a word or two, I went on through to the billiard-room. I looked at the clock in the study as I passed, and it was exactly ten. I can't say, though, at just what time the general alarm was given; I should think less than a half hour later."

"I can tell you," said Gilbert. "When I concluded to go home, I looked between the portiéres into Mr. Maxwell's study, and it was twenty minutes past ten. Mr. Maxwell was nodding over his paper; he is a little deaf, so he probably didn't hear me.

"At any rate, he didn't look up. Then I went immediately upstairs, and it could not have been more than two minutes before I called Dr. Sheldon."

"All this is of interest, and I thank you," said Detective Hunt. "Although, as you say, since there is no criminal to discover, there is small use of collecting evidence."

"Queer chap, isn't he?" I said to Gilbert, as the detective went away.

"Yes, but I think he's clever."

"I don't; if there were any occasion for detective work on this case, I believe I could give him cards and spades, and then beat him at his own game."

"Perhaps you could," said Gilbert, but he spoke without interest.

There was plenty for all to do that day. I had expected to return to New York, but both Mr. Maxwell and Miss Miranda begged me to stay with them till after the funeral. As there was no reason for my immediate presence in the city, I was glad to be of service to my good friends. I assisted Mr. Maxwell to write letters to the various relatives, and together we looked over poor Philip's effects. The boy had no business papers to speak of, for he had no money except what was given him by his uncle, and apparently he kept no account of its expenditures.

"I paid all his bills," said Mr. Maxwell, in explanation of this, "and kept the receipts. I allowed Philip such ready cash as he wanted, and, I may say, I never stinted him. Whatever his recent trouble may have been, it could not have arisen from lack of funds."

"Unless he had been speculating privately," I suggested.

"I can't think so," replied his uncle. "Philip wasn't that sort, and, too, had that been the case, we would surely find papers of some sort to show it."

This was true enough, and as Philip's papers consisted entirely of such documents as scented notes addressed in feminine hands, letters from college chums, circulars of outing goods and cigars, and old dance-orders, I agreed that there was no indication of financial trouble.

Mr. Maxwell was very careful and methodical in his search. In a business-like way he went rapidly through the papers, replacing the contents of each pigeon-hole or drawer after rapidly looking them over. He showed no curiosity concerning the social notes or the circulars, but seemed searching for some letter or document that might throw light on Philip's recent despondency.

"It was about two weeks ago that Philip began to act differently," mused Mr. Maxwell, as he scanned the dates on various papers, "but I can find nothing here that would show any reason for it. The poor boy must have had some secret trouble; and doubtless, after all, it was either directly or indirectly concerned with Mildred Leslie."

The old gentleman seemed almost relieved that no letters or documents were found that showed a reason for Philip's trouble. And I could understand this, for surely it was better that a love affair should be the explanation, than some secret and perhaps dishonorable reason.

The desk we had been searching was in Philip's dressing-room, a small room off his bedroom. With the systematic thoroughness that was characteristic of him, Mr. Maxwell opened the drawers of the chiffonier, and examined the contents of a few small cabinets and boxes that stood about. He even glanced over the crumpled papers that were in the waste-basket, and then declared himself satisfied that we could find no written evidence bearing upon the secret of the boy's recent strange behavior.

Mr. Maxwell returned to his study, and I went for a stroll with Irene Gardiner. The girl looked so pale and wan, that I hoped a brisk walk would do her good.

"Do you believe in the 'accidental' theory?" she asked, as soon as we were started.

"No," I replied. "Philip was too well used to firearms to shoot anybody accidentally, or allow anyone to shoot him. But I now fully believe in Mr. Maxwell's theory that the boy's brain was temporarily affected, and that he shot himself in a moment of insanity."

"But if he shot himself first, how did he then shoot Mildred?"

"I've puzzled over that, I confess, and I think he shot her first—as I said—not being responsible for his actions. And then, overcome by grief at what he had done, he killed himself in his sudden despair."

"Yes," said Irene. "I suppose that must have been the way of it. But, granting all that, I don't see how Mildred came to have the pistol in her hand."

"Nor I. It is all most mysterious. Let us hope that Mildred will soon recover, and then we will know all."

"Mr. King, I suppose you will think very hardly of me, but I have looked at this matter in all lights, and I want to ask you if this isn't a possible case. Mightn't Philip have shot Mildred, and, since she is not very severely wounded, might she not have then snatched the pistol from him and shot at him in return."

I looked at Miss Gardiner in amazement. I felt horrified that she should imagine this, and yet there was a shadow of plausibility in it.

"It seems almost impossible," I said slowly, "that a wounded girl could have energy enough to secure a pistol and shoot her assailant. And yet, I admit, I can think of no other way to explain Miss Leslie's repeated expressions of grieved amazement that Philip should have shot her."

"You don't think it possible, then, that Mildred may not be as unconscious as she seems, and that she is making this repeated statement for reasons of her own."

"Miss Gardiner!" I exclaimed, now thoroughly aroused, "I am surprised at you. Even if you suspect Miss Leslie of absolute crime, pray give the poor girl the benefit of the doubt until she can defend herself, or—is beyond all need of defense."

"You do me injustice," said Irene, raising her head haughtily. "My logical mind necessitates the consideration of every possible solution of this puzzle. I look upon Mildred impersonally, merely as one of the actors in a tragic drama."

"You have indeed a logical mind," I said coldly, "if you can entirely eliminate the personal element from your estimate of Miss Leslie."

"I see no reason why I should not. I judge her fairly, and without prejudice. But I fail to see why the ravings of a mind affected by the consequences of an anesthetic should be accepted as unquestioned truth."

"On the contrary, the revelations made by a brain just reviving from the unconsciousness produced by ether, are conceded by all medical authorities invariably to be true statements. Many secrets have been revealed in this way."

"That fact is new to me," said Irene thoughtfully, "and it is very interesting. I am always willing to accept authoritative facts, but I decline to accept unproved theories."

"At any rate," I ventured, "you have no word of blame for Philip." She turned flashing eyes toward me, and in a moment I realized the situation. She was in the grip of two strong emotions. Grief for the man she had loved, and jealousy of her rival.

"Never speak of him to me!" she exclaimed. "I claim that much consideration from you."

"And you shall certainly receive it," I said gently. "But, on the other hand, let me beg of you not to do an innocent girl an injustice, which your better nature will surely regret later."

Irene looked at me.

She had never seemed more beautiful, and her wonderful eyes expressed contrition, gratitude, and a deep and hopeless sadness.

She held out her hand.

"I thank you," she said, "you have saved me from a grave mistake."

Still I didn't understand her, but I realized she was beginning to fascinate me in her mysterious way, and I abruptly turned our steps toward home.

When we reached Maxwell Chimneys, we found Dr. Sheldon, and the Whitings, with Mr. Maxwell and Miss Miranda in the study.

Evidently something had happened. Each one looked excited; Mr. Maxwell was writing rapidly, and Tom Whiting was hastily turning the leaves of the telephone book. "What is it?" I inquired. "Is Mildred…"

"No," said Dr. Sheldon, "Miss Leslie is no worse. On the contrary, she is much better. Her mind is entirely cleared, and she talks rationally, though I am not willing she should be questioned much as yet. I am very glad you have come, for there is a new and startling development in the case, and there is much to be done."

"What is it?" I asked.

"Simply this. Miss Leslie, being perfectly rational, you understand, says that neither she nor Philip fired any shots at all. They were both shot by an intruder who came in at the library window."

"But," I exclaimed, "then what did she mean by saying 'He shot me!' in such a grieved tone?"

"She tells us," said Dr. Sheldon, "that those were the last words uttered by Philip as he fell, and that they rang in her brain to the exclusion of all else. That is why she repeated them, parrot-like, during her unconsciousness."

"This changes the whole situation," said I, thinking rapidly.

"It does," said Mr. Maxwell. "It is now a case for a detective." Then he added, in a manly way, "I am sorry I spoke so shortly to Mr. Hunt this morning, and I am ready to tell him so, and to ask him to return and help us."

"But what—" I began.

"You know all that we do," interrupted the doctor. "If Miss Leslie is questioned further, or in any way excited at present, I will not answer for the consequences. My first duty is to my patient.

"This afternoon, and in my presence, she may be interviewed by someone who can do it gently and discreetly. Tomorrow, in all probability, she will be quite herself, and may be questioned by a detective or any one empowered by Mr. Maxwell."

And with this, we were obliged to be content.

VIII: The Inquest

THE situation was indeed changed. My latent detective instinct was now fully roused, and I determined to do all I could toward solving the mystery.

I said as much to Mr. Maxwell, and he thanked me for my sympathy and interest. He also asked whether I thought Mr. Hunt a skilled detective, or whether I advised sending to New York for a more expert man. This annoyed me, for it proved that he considered my services as well-meant, but not especially valuable. However, I showed no irritation, and answered simply that I thought Mr. Hunt quite capable of discovering all that could be discovered.

"You see," I went on, "we are at a disadvantage in having lost so many hours already. Had we known last night there was an intruder from outside, we could perhaps have caught him. As it is, he has probably made good his escape."

"That is true," said Mr. Maxwell with a sigh.

"But we must do our best, and leave no stone unturned in our endeavor to find Philip's assailant."

Miss Maxwell also agreed to this. "Peter," she said, and her look at me was pathetic, "you will help us, won't you? You loved Philip, I know; and you are clever and intelligent. Can't you help Mr. Hunt, and between you find the villain who murdered our boy?"

The usually timid and gentle lady was stirred, as I had never seen her, by her righteous indignation. I was touched by her confidence in me, and I assured her that such capability as I possessed should be devoted toward the tracking of the criminal. I determined to go at once to the library, the scene of the crime, and make a thorough search for clues before Mr. Hunt should arrive. All the detective literature I had ever read, had taught me that it is next to impossible for a human being to enter a room and go out again, without leaving a trace of some sort, though visible only to a trained detective. So to the library I went, and subjected the room and all its contents to a minute and systematic scrutiny. Contrary to all precedent, literary and reportorial, I found nothing.

Again I went over the room, even more diligently, remembering Sherlock Holmes' wise advice to discriminate carefully between vital and incidental clues.

But, alas, I could find neither, except the very doubtful one of a small and shiny black spangle, a tiny disk, which might have fallen from the trimmings of some lady's gown. I remembered no one who had worn such a decoration the night before, but then, I take little note of ladies' dress. In lieu of anything more interesting, I put the spangle carefully away in my note-book, and proceeded with my examinations.

All to no purpose.

The room had been put in order by the servants that morning—dusted, and possibly swept—so it was absurd to look for anything on the floor or furniture.

Sighing to think of the opportunities we had lost, I turned my attention to the window by which the intruder must have entered. It was a long French window reaching from floor to ceiling. It was in three divisions, each of which was really a door, and opened out on the balcony, which as I have said, ran around both sides and the front of the house without barrier.

The panes were of ground glass, in a diamond pattern; and I knew that at night, with lights inside the room, an outsider might look in through the glass unseen by those within.

I opened the middle door, stepped out on the balcony, and endeavored to scrutinize in a scientific way.

Signs of a scuffle there certainly were.

Just outside the library window, in the dust of the balcony, I observed many long, sweeping marks, that had every appearance of being the tracks of men who scraped their feet around in a wrestle, or struggle of some sort. From the shape of these streaks in the dust, I could not gather the size of the shoes that made them, nor the style of their toes; but as even the paint of the balcony floor was scratched by the marks, I felt sure that a tussle of some sort had taken place there.

I looked for a continuation of these tracks, but found none, save the scratches that were to be seen everywhere over the balcony floor. As many people had walked there the night before, this was of no importance, but unless someone had danced a clog dance outside the library window, I saw no reason for changing my first conclusion.

I found nothing else of note, save two more of those little black spangles—one in the outside library blind, and another farther front on the balcony. These I put away with my first one, determined to find out who wore such trimmings the evening before.

By this time Mr. Hunt had arrived. The coroner had come, too, bringing his jury, for it had been decided to begin the inquest that very afternoon.

How strange it seemed, to hold an inquest in Miss Miranda's stately drawing-room!

But that was not more strange than realizing that Philip's dead body lay upstairs, and that we had not the faintest idea whose hand wrought this evil.

I paused in the library to talk to Mr. Hunt. He was not mysterious and uncommunicative like the regulation detective, but was frankly at his wits' end.

When I saw this, and knew that I was similarly unenlightened, I wondered if I had done wisely in advising Mr. Maxwell against getting a man from the city.

"Very little to work on, eh, Hunt?" I said.

"Just about nothing at all," he said, moodily staring at the carpet. "Look here, Mr. King, who is that foreigner staying here?"

"The Earl of Clarendon? Oh, he's a noble Britisher, all right. Don't try to stir up anything against him!"

"I'm not; don't be absurd. But, have they known him long?"

"When Mr. Alexander Maxwell and Miss Miranda traveled abroad a few years ago, I believe he entertained them in London, or at his country house. He's the real thing, Hunt, don't get any notions about that."

"I can't get any notions anywhere; there's nothing to work on."

"But the inquest may bring out some important facts."

"I doubt it. If anyone knew anything, he would have told it at once. Why shouldn't he? We are all of one interest. The deed was doubtless done by a burglar who was trying to effect an entrance, and who was frightened away by his own shots."

"Well," I responded, "I'm willing to suspend judgment until I have something more definite to base my opinions on. Come, let us go downstairs."

A crowd had assembled in the lower rooms, for the inquest was, in a way, a public function. I was sure the Maxwells were terribly annoyed at this invasion of their beautiful home, but I was also sure that such thoughts were swallowed up in their eagerness to discover and punish the murderer of Philip.

Mr. Billings was calm and business-like. He had impaneled his jury, and was already examining the first witness. Mr. Maxwell's own lawyer was present, also the district attorney and several other gentlemen of legal aspect who were strangers to me.

The first witness was Gilbert Crane.

To my surprise he appeared agitated and ill at ease. In one way, this was not astonishing, for, as the first one to discover the tragedy, his testimony would be of great importance. But he had been so cool and self-possessed all day that I couldn't understand his present demeanor.

"Will you tell us," said the coroner, not unkindly, "the circumstances which led to your going to the library last evening?"

"I was alone in the billiard-room," said Gilbert.

"I had been there alone for some time, as I was troubled and did not care to join the merry crowd in the drawing-room. I heard Mr. King come downstairs, go into Mr. Maxwell's study and talk to him for a few moments. After this I heard Mr. King tell Mr. Maxwell that Philip Maxwell and Miss Leslie were in the library.

"After this, Mr. King walked through the room I was in, but we said nothing to each other, and he went on to the drawing-room. I stayed exactly where I was for some time longer, and then I concluded I would go home.

"Not wishing to make my adieux to the guests, I thought I would merely say good night to Mr. Maxwell. I lifted the portiére and looked into his study, but as he was asleep, I thought I wouldn't disturb him, but would just run upstairs for my banjo, and then slip away unnoticed.

"I went upstairs and I admit it was curiosity concerning the two people inside that led me to pause and look toward the library door. I heard no sound of voices, so I took another step or two in that direction, and, looking, saw Philip's figure stretched on the floor.

"Then, of course, I went into the room. It has no door, and the portieres were but partly drawn. Seeing what was evidently a serious accident of some sort, I immediately ran down-stairs and called Dr. Sheldon to the scene."

"You saw no one else in the room?"

"N—no," said Gilbert, but he seemed to hesitate.

"You are quite sure?" asked the coroner.

"I am positive I saw no one else in the room," said Gilbert, decidedly this time.

"Can you fix the time of your going upstairs?"

"I can. When I looked into Mr. Maxwell's study, I noticed by his large clock that it was twenty minutes after ten. In less than a minute after that I was upstairs."

"That will do," said Mr. Billings, and Gilbert was dismissed.

Dr. Sheldon was called next, and testified that he had responded immediately to Mr. Crane's call, and on reaching the library found Philip Maxwell's dead body on the floor, and Miss Leslie, wounded and unconscious, a few feet away.

"She was shot?" asked the coroner.

"Yes, shot in the shoulder. She had fallen, and in so doing had hit her temple. This rendered her unconscious. I extracted the ball, and found it to be a thirty-eight caliber. The revolver found in Miss Leslie's hand is also thirty-eight caliber."

"And has the ball been extracted from Mr. Philip Maxwell's body?"

"Yes; that is also a thirty-eight caliber. He was shot through the heart, and must have died instantly."

"In your opinion, how long had he been dead, when you examined the body?"

"Not long, as the body was still warm. Not more than half an hour at the most."

"The pistol found in Miss Leslie's hand, and which is now in my possession," said Mr. Billings, "has two empty chambers. In view of Miss Leslie's statement that the shooting was done by a person who came in by the window, it would seem that the intruder might have placed the weapon in Miss Leslie's hand after she was wounded. In your opinion, Dr. Sheldon, would this be possible?"

"Possible, yes, but highly improbable, as I myself took the pistol from her hand, and she was holding it in a tight grasp. This would scarcely have been the case, had it been thrust into her hand while she lay unconscious."

"We will not pursue this line of investigation further, until we can hear Miss Leslie's story," said Mr. Billings. "Dr. Sheldon, you are excused."

Mr. Maxwell's testimony was merely to the effect that he had spent the evening in the drawing room until about half past nine, at which time he went to his study, and remained there, reading and occasionally dozing, until he had been told the dreadful news.

He corroborated my statement about my looking in on him at ten o'clock, though he didn't notice the time, and he said that he neither saw nor heard Gilbert Crane look in later. Asked if he heard any shots, he said he did not, owing, doubtless, to his deafness, and the fact that he was asleep part of the time. He was excused, and Mr. Billings then inquired if anyone had heard any shots.

We who were in the drawing-room during the half-hour between ten and ten-thirty (when the murder was judged to have taken place) declared we heard no shots; and this was but natural, as the library was upstairs and some distance away, and the music was, at that time, of a noisy variety.

Gilbert Crane said he heard no shots, but said that he was so deeply immersed in his own thoughts, that he doubted if he would have heard a cannon fired.

Then Miss Maxwell's gentle voice was heard, saying:

"I heard two shots, and they were fired at exactly ten o'clock."

"This is most important, madam," said the coroner. "Will you kindly take the witness chair?"

Then Miss Miranda testified that she was in her own room preparing for bed. Her doors were closed, and the water was running for her bath, so that she could not hear distinctly, but at ten o'clock she heard two sounds that seemed to her like pistol shots. At the time, however, she hardly thought they were shots, but she opened her hall door and looked out. Seeing nothing unusual, and hearing the gay music downstairs, she assumed it was the slamming of doors or some other unimportant noise, and so thought no more of it, until informed of what had happened.

"This, then," said Mr. Billings, "fixes the firing of the two shots at ten o'clock. That coincides with your diagnosis, Dr. Sheldon?"

"Yes, sir," said the doctor.

"I went upstairs at about half past ten, and found the body still warm."

"It is fortunate that we are able thus to fix the time so accurately," said the coroner, "as it may be helpful in discovering the criminal."

IX: Further Testimony

THE next witness called was Irene Gardiner.

For some unaccountable reason, I trembled as I saw her take the stand. There was no knowing what sort of an impression this strange girl might create, and there were certain bits of evidence which I would feel sorry to have brought out in reference to her.

"Where were you between ten and ten-thirty last evening?" asked Mr. Billings.

Although the tone was courteous, the question had somewhat the sound of a challenge.

"On the upper balcony," replied Irene, her head held high, and her red lips curled in a haughty expression.

"Which part of the balcony?" The coroner's voice was a little more gentle.

"The south end of the east side."

That was where I had left her when I came downstairs at ten o'clock. The library opened on the southern end of the west balcony.

"Were you there alone? "

"Mr. King was with me part of the time. Also there were others in different parts of the balcony. After Mr. King left me I was alone."

"Were not the others you mentioned there?"

"I don't know; I could see no one from where I sat."

"How long did you remain there?"

"I cannot tell the exact time. When I came into the house again, I was met by Mr. King, who told me what had happened, and asked me to break the news to Miss Maxwell."

"While sitting on the balcony alone did you see any strangers, or any one, around the grounds, or on the driveway?"

"None."

"Did you stay in the same place all the time you were on the balcony, after Mr. King left you?"

"No—that is, yes."

"What do you mean by that answer?"

"I walked a few steps back and forth."

"Not around the corner into the north side?"

"N—no. Not so far as that."

As Irene made this statement, her face grew ashen pale, and I thought I saw her glance in the direction of Gilbert Crane. But I was not sure of this, and I was most anxious to make all allowance for the girl, who was certainly pitiably nervous and disturbed.

"You are quite sure, Miss Gardiner, that you did not walk round on the north or west sides of the balcony until the time you came into the house?"

"Quite certain," said Irene, but her voice was so low as scarcely to be heard, and her eyes were cast down.

I didn't know what to make of her strange manner, and just then I chanced to look at Gilbert Crane. To my surprise, he was equally pale and agitated in appearance. No one else seemed to notice this, so I kept my own counsel concerning it.

Miss Gardiner was dismissed, and the Earl of Clarendon was next called.

Mr. Billings inquired rather definitely as to the title and pedigree of the English nobleman, and, seemingly satisfied with the replies, he asked the witness to tell what he could of the tragedy.

"I can tell very little," the Earl responded. "I was dancing with a young lady in the drawing room, when I heard Mr. Crane announce from the doorway that somebody had been shot. I realized at once that unless restrained, the guests would all rush to the scene. I took the young lady who was with me to a sofa, and then I spoke to all the people at once, advising them to remain in the drawing-room. I may have taken upon myself undue authority, but I did it in an endeavor to avoid a scene of confusion. After a time, we all learned what had happened, and of course the guests for the most part went away at once."

"Where had you been just before the dance during which you heard the news?"

"I had been on the lower veranda."

"With whom?"

"I was alone. I wanted to smoke a cigarette, and I strolled round the verandas, toward the back of the house."

"On the same side of the house as the library, upstairs?"

"Yes, the same side."

"Did you see any person or persons other than the guests of the house?"

"No, that is, not that I could distinguish. But I saw a motor car which came swiftly up the drive, passed me, and went on round the house."

"Did you notice the car especially?"

"I gave it little thought, as it might have been bringing or taking guests, or might have had to do with the caterers or servants."

"Can you describe the car?"

"Though I didn't see it clearly, it gave me the impression of being long and low, and of a gray color. Also, it was going rapidly."

"That would scarcely seem to indicate the motor vehicle of a caterer."

"Nor do I say that it did. I have no reason to give the car any thought whatever; and I have merely a memory of the car passing me as I finished my cigarette and returned to the dancing-room. I can tell you no more of it."

"You didn't notice its occupants?"

"No; nor could I see them distinctly. I fancy, however, there were three or four men in it; but again, that is merely an impression I gained from the fleeting vision. I turned away from it, even as it passed me."

After a few more inquiries the Earl was dismissed, and other witnesses followed. None was important, in the sense of throwing any further light on the incidents of the evening before.

The Whitings and other guests who had been in the drawing-room, simply repeated what was already known.

The servants had heard no shots, but as they were at that time in the outer kitchen, busily engaged in preparations for supper, that was not surprising. The coachman and gardener had rooms in the barn buildings, and said they heard nothing unusual until notified of the catastrophe. There were now no more witnesses to be heard from, save the most important one of all, Mildred Leslie. Dr. Sheldon consented that she should be interviewed, but requested a delay of an hour or so.

The coroner, therefore, announced a brief recess, and as we had all given our testimony, we were not required to remain in the drawing-room with the jury and the officials. But as we were all more than anxious to be on hand to hear Mildred's statement, we did not drift far away.

Gilbert Crane and I strolled on the front lawn, smoking and discussing the inquest. I was most curious to know the reason of his extraordinary hesitation at some points of his testimony, but not caring to inquire directly, I resolved to find out in a roundabout way.

"What did you think of Miss Gardiner's testimony?" I asked.

"I think the poor girl was so agitated she did not know what she was saying," he replied somewhat shortly, and as if he did not wish to dwell on the subject.

But I was not to be turned from it.

"It is not like Miss Gardiner," I went on, "to lose her poise in an emergency. She is usually so calm and self-possessed."

"I do not consider Miss Gardiner's a calm temperament," said Crane; "I think she is decidedly emotional."

"Emotional, yes; but she has a wonderful control over her emotions. And aside from that, she positively contradicted herself this morning. I wonder if she did walk around to the west side of the balcony and look in at the library window."

This was mere idle speculation on my part, but it had a strange effect on Gilbert Crane.

"What do you mean?" he cried angrily. "Are you insinuating anything against Miss Gardiner's veracity, or do you perhaps consider her implicated in the affair?"

"I have no thought of Miss Gardiner, save such as are most honorable and loyal," I said; "but, by the way, Crane, what sort of a gown did she wear last night?"

"I don't know, I'm sure. I'm no authority on ladies' dress. I never notice their furbelows."

Somehow, the emphasis with which he said this made me think he was overdoing it, and that perhaps he was not so ignorant as he wished me to suppose. But I had no desire to antagonize him, so I dropped the discussion of Irene altogether.

He was amiable enough then, and we returned to the house, chatting affably.

Determined to settle a certain point, I went in search of Miss Maxwell, and found that good lady in the study with her brother.

"Miss Miranda," I said, without subterfuge, "what sort of a gown did Miss Gardiner wear last evening?"

"Irene? Why, she had on a lovely rose-colored silk-gauze—a sort of pineapple material."

"Was it trimmed with black spangles?"

"No, Peter, it was all pin."

'She didn't inquire why I wished to know; indeed, I think she scarcely realized what she was talking about, for she spoke almost automatically. I understood this, for all day she had seemed dazed and bewildered, and unable to concentrate her mind.

"What is it, Peter?" asked Mr. Maxwell, "have you learned anything new?"

They were very pathetic, these two old people, who had lost their only link to the world of youth and happiness, but the brother seemed to me especially to be pitied. Owing to his deafness, he heard nothing except what was directly addressed to him, and was naturally anxious for any side-lights on the affair.

"No, sir," I replied, "nothing new. But I think we shall soon hear Miss Leslie's statement, and then we will know where to begin our work."

"Leave no stone unturned, my boy; call on me for any money you may need, and spare no trouble or expense in your efforts. You're something of a detective yourself, aren't you, Peter? Can't you ferret this thing out?"

"I mean to try, sir," I replied. "But we have lost so much time, and there is so little evidence, I have small hope of success."

"Have you any theory or suspicion?" asked Mr. Maxwell.

I couldn't tell him of my finding the spangles, and I hadn't a thought of Irene that could deserve the name suspicion, but he seemed to notice my hesitation.

"You needn't answer that," he said in a kind way, "only remember this, my boy. Be careful how you proceed on suspicion, unless your proof is pretty positive. Trace your clues carefully, and don't let them mislead you."

It seemed as if he must have read my thought—or had he too found some spangles?

Well, at any rate, I would follow his advice, and be very careful before I let even my own thoughts doubt Irene.

And now we heard the people coming down from upstairs, and all hastened back to the drawing-room.

Since Mildred's assertion that Philip was killed by an intruder, the district attorney had been called in, and had of course attended the whole inquest.

He was a Mr. Edwards, and seemed to be an alert and intelligent man.

Like the rest of us, he eagerly awaited the expected statement, and when the Coroner rose, the general excitement, though subdued, was intense.

X: Mildred's Strange Story

"I WILL call the next witness," the coroner announced, "Miss Mildred Leslie."

There was an expectant hush all over the room, as Mildred came through the door, supported on one side by the white-capped nurse and on the other by Doctor Sheldon. Edith Whiting followed, looking very anxious, and, it seemed to me, annoyed. I knew she thought her sister was not well enough to go through this ordeal, but I knew, too, that it must be gone through, for of course this testimony was the most important of all.

Mr. Billings looked at his witness almost with consternation, when he saw how weak and fragile she appeared, and he spoke in very gentle tones.

"Miss Leslie," he said, "I will detain you no longer than is absolutely necessary. Will you tell, in your own words, the story of what occurred last evening in the library?"

Mildred stirred uneasily in the big chair, where the nurse had placed her, and grasped nervously at the hand of Miss Lathrop as she sat beside her. The nurse, the doctor and Edith Whiting were all looking anxiously at Milly as if afraid of her collapse. But seeming to nerve herself, with an effort, the girl began:

"Philip Maxwell and I were in the library, and had been there some time, when a man appeared."

"Wait a moment, Miss Leslie," interrupted Mr. Billings.

"I must ask for more details. Excuse me, but on what subjects were you and Mr. Maxwell conversing?"

"Do I have to tell that?" and Milly smiled at the coroner, looking almost like her old self again.

"I'm sorry to annoy you,"—Mr. Billings was certainly under the spell of Milly's smile,—"but I must ask you to."

"Well, then," and Milly pouted a little, "he was asking me to marry him."

"And you said?"

"Oh, I refused to. I had refused him lots of times before. He knew I didn't care for him,— that way."

"He knew then, that his was a hopeless suit?"

"He certainly did."

"Why, then, did he continue to insist upon it?"

"Well, he said that he had something to tell me that would make me change my mind."

"What was it?"

"I don't know, I'm sure. Before he had time to tell me, that awful man came, an…"

Milly put her hands up to her face, and swayed from side to side, as her thoughts flew back to the dreadful scene. Miss Lathrop put an arm around her, and offered her smelling-salts, while Edith Whiting whispered to the doctor, who only shook his head.

Indeed, all the members of the household sympathized with the poor little girl, suffering from shock and real illness. But the coroner and the District Attorney were determined to get her story if possible.

"Rest a few moments, Miss Leslie," said Mr. Billings, "and then try to continue."

"It's an outrage," murmured old Mr. Maxwell; "it's a shame to torment the poor child!"

"But better to get it over at once," said Lord Clarendon, who was gravely listening to the proceedings of the inquest.

I liked the Earl's manner; though solicitous for Mildred's comfort, he seemed to desire that the inquiry should go on as steadily as possible, toward the discovery of the truth.

"Never mind the intruder at present, Miss Leslie," went on the coroner. "What did you do then?"

"Nothing. I was so paralyzed with fright, that I couldn't move,—I couldn't even scream."

"And what did Mr. Maxwell do?"

"He seemed paralyzed too. It seemed like minutes, but I don't suppose it was, that we three stood there, looking at each other."

"And then?"

"And then," Mildred gasped as if for breath, but gripping the arms of her chair tightly, she went steadily on; "and then, Philip pulled open the top drawer of the table-desk, and grabbed out a pistol. He raised it to aim at the man, but at the same time, he said, in a low, moaning voice, 'Oh, to think he would shoot me!'"

"Then, Miss Leslie, you think Mr. Maxwell knew who shot him?"

"I think he must have known, from the way he spoke. But the man was a stranger to me. He had—"

"You may describe him later. Go on with your connected story, please."

"Well, when I saw Philip take his pistol, I had a wild desire to prevent either of the men from shooting. I suppose I was almost crazed by fright, and scarcely knew what I was doing. But my only thought was to attack the man who was threatening Philip, and so I threw…"

Mildred stopped suddenly in her recital. Both nurse and doctor leaned forward to see if she were exhausted, but she was not. She seemed to have been struck by a sudden thought, and hesitating what to say next.

I chanced to look at the Earl and found him regarding Milly intently. He had a curious look on his face, and his tightly interlaced fingers were the first sign of nervousness he had shown. He did not glance my way, but kept his gaze fixed on Milly's face, as if trying to attract her attention. If so, he succeeded, for she turned slowly and looked in his direction. She gazed straight at him for a moment, and then tossed her head with a willful little gesture peculiar to herself.

Then she turned again to the coroner.

"Proceed, Miss Leslie. You threw something at this intruder?"

"Yes; I thought if I could hit him I might prevent his shooting. I snatched up a heavy cut glass inkstand full of ink, from the desk, and threw it at him. I don't know whether it hit him or not, but the next second I picked up a bronze horse,— a paper-weight,—from the desk and threw that at him, too."

Milly was talking rapidly, and growing very much excited. Her cheeks burned, her eyes were big and shiny, and her fingers picked nervously at the arms of her chair.

Mr. Billings looked at her curiously. "You threw these heavy missiles at him?"

"Yes, I did! and it didn't take as long to do it, as it does to tell it, for my hands fairly flew. I couldn't speak or make a sound, but I felt impelled to act!"

"You are sure you threw these things, Miss Leslie?" and the coroner's tone was emphatically one of incredulity.

"Of course I'm sure!" she declared, angrily.

"And did any of these things hit him?"

"I don't know, I tell you! It's all a blur to me – the whole scene. But I remember that Philip and the man paid no attention to me, but stood with their pistols pointed at each other. Then Philip said again, in that moaning voice, 'to think he would shoot me!' and just then the man fired."

"With what result?"

"Philip fell backward, and as he fell, his pistol dropped from his hand onto the desk." Mildred's excitement had died away, and she spoke now in a tense, low voice, and seemed to be holding herself together by a desperate effort. Her eyes had a far-away look, and she went steadily on.

"I don't know what gave me courage, for I had never so much as touched a revolver before; but I suppose I was nerved up by fright, and I picked up Philip's pistol and aimed at the man, myself. With that," and Mildred's voice sank to a whisper, "he turned his own pistol toward me,—I heard the report,—and I remember falling forward. I remember nothing more."

There was a silence as Milly stopped speaking. Everyone felt the horror of the recital; everyone realized the mystery surrounding the crime. Who could have been desirous of killing both these young people?

I glanced round at our household group. The old people, Alexander Maxwell and his sister, sat hand in hand, their heads bowed with grief. Mr. Maxwell, I felt sure, had not heard all of the evidence, but of course it would be repeated to him afterwards. And perhaps after all it were well if he could be spared the harrowing details. Miss Maxwell sat with trembling lips, and though her heart was breaking, she controlled herself in her effort to be a comfort and stay to her brother.

Irene Gardiner was listening to Mildred with rapt attention and alert intelligence. She had not missed a word of all the inquiry, and I knew she was storing up in her memory every bit of testimony to be coldly considered afterward. Her air was judicial, and her calm impressed me unpleasantly. I admired the girl so much, that I resented this calculating side of her nature, which always jarred upon me.

Edith Whiting and her husband were more concerned lest the occasion prove too much for Mildred's strength and nerves, than they were in the outcome of the inquest.

The Earl sat with his eyes on the floor, now, and occasionally shook his head, as if dissatisfied with his own thoughts. Gilbert Crane was very nervous, and fidgeted incessantly with his watch chain or a lead pencil or any small object he could lay hands on.

But the coroner was continuing his questions.

"Miss Leslie," he said, "you have given a very clear and coherent statement. Now if you will describe the intruder, we will not disturb you further today."

"I can't describe him very much, except to say that he wore motoring clothes. A big coat, a cap with a visor, and goggles which covered most of his face."

"Not the lower part of his face?"

"No, but his large collar was turned up, and buttoned across in a way to hide his mouth and chin."

"Would you recognize him if you saw him again?"

"I'm sure I could not. The clothes were not peculiar in any way. Just such as all men wear motoring."

"Was it a fur coat?"

"No, not that kind. A sort of thick cloth, I think,—of medium color, but rather light than dark."

"And the cap?"

"I think that was light, too, but I couldn't say for certain."

"Did he wear gloves?"

Mildred looked perplexed.

"I can't say; I rather think he did, but my eyes rested on the pistol,—it seemed to fascinate me,—and I thought only of how I could prevent him from firing it."

"That is all, Miss Leslie," said Mr. Billings, and Mildred was allowed to be taken back to her own room. All! I should think it was enough! I felt as if I must get away to think things over by myself.

I rushed from the room and out on the veranda, where I found a secluded corner. What sort of a story had Mildred told, and why? For the doctor had sworn she was perfectly sane and rational, and quite capable of describing the affair. Why, then, did she say she threw an inkstand full of ink and a bronze horse at the intruder, when I, who had so carefully searched the room for clues, found no traces of ink? And, moreover, I especially remembered seeing that bronze horse on the desk when I first entered the library after Gilbert Crane had given the alarm!

Not for a moment did I doubt Mildred's good faith in the matter. It would be too absurd to think of her making such statements if they were not true. And yet how could they be true? How could anyone throw an inkstand full of ink, and not leave black spots somewhere? How could anyone throw a heavy bronze paper-weight, and, being shot a moment later, restore the bronze to its place on the table? Clearly she must be laboring under an hallucination regarding these things. Probably she so strongly desired to throw the inkstand or the horse that she really believed she did throw them.

Yes, that must be it. There was no other plausible explanation of her words.

XI: The Black Spangles

AS was to be expected, the jury returned a verdict of willful murder against a person unknown; and I concluded from this, that they had accepted Mildred's story as true.

And if so, then the main thing now, was to find the man in the automobile clothes. He must be someone whom Philip knew and recognized in spite of the goggles. He must have come in an automobile, for men do not walk around the country in such attire. But Miss Gardiner on the balcony commanded a view of the entrance and driveway, and she had seen no one enter the grounds. Possibly then he had come from a distance, had left his machine at some point nearby, and had approached the house secretly and on foot. But how had he gained an entrance? The servants had not let him in. He couldn't have come in by the front door without being seen. The conservatory door was always locked at night.

Oh, well, while all these things were true, still there were many windows by which he might have entered, and slipped upstairs unseen. Then he could have gone out on the balcony through the little cross-hall and so reached the library window. Or, he might have climbed to the balcony by means of a veranda pillar. An agile man could easily do this—still, not so easily if dressed in a bulky automobile coat.

It was mysterious enough, but of course the first thing to do was to look for traces. If I had only known sooner that there was an intruder to be looked for, how much better a chance we should have had of finding him.

But there was no use crying over spilled milk, so I started at once to look carefully at the veranda pillars. There I found myself forestalled.

Mr. Hunt and Gilbert Crane were already examining them.

"Any scratches?" said I.

"Plenty of old ones," said Mr. Hunt, "but none that seems to have been made as recently as last night."

"How about automobile tracks?"

"There are any number of those, all over the drive; but as several people came in automobiles last night, they mean nothing definite."

"What do you make of those marks on the balcony floor that look as if made by scuffling feet?"

"They may be the marks of a scuffle," said Mr. Hunt, "or it may be that someone stood for some time looking in at the library window. A nervous person standing there might move about in a manner to leave just such traces."

For some unaccountable reason these remarks of Mr. Hunt's seemed to disturb Gilbert Crane. He turned pale and was about to speak, then set his lips firmly, and turned silently away.

"There is one circumstance that ought to be explained," I said, speaking to Mr. Hunt, and hoping that Crane would leave us. But Gilbert turned back and seemed anxious to know what I was about to say. I watched him closely as I went on, though addressing my remarks directly to Mr. Hunt.

"I found these bits of evidence this morning," I said, taking my note-book from my pocket. "They may not be vital clues, but anything found in the library is of interest."

Even before I opened my note-book Crane showed signs of agitation which he tried vainly to suppress. His white, frightened face and his clenched hands showed that he feared the disclosure. Still watching him covertly, I produced the three black spangles.

"Do you recognize these?"

"No," said Mr. Hunt, "what are they, and where did they come from?"

"Do you recognize them?" I said, turning suddenly to Crane.

"No!" he declared, but with such emphasis that I doubted him. "But they can't possibly be of any importance."

"Perhaps not," I returned, "but I picked them up in the library, and on the balcony, and one piece I disengaged from the catch of the library window shutter."

"Well," said Gilbert Crane, trying to speak naturally, "and what does that prove to you?"

"It doesn't prove anything," I said slowly, "but it is a peculiar coincidence that they should be found just where the intruder of last night must have stood."

"Meaning that it might have been a woman?" said Hunt, quickly.

"Possibly," I returned. "But none of the ladies were on the upper balcony last evening at ten o'clock, except Miss Gardiner, and she declares that she was not in the library or on the west balcony at all."

"She says that?" said Hunt. looking up sharply, while Gilbert Crane looked more distressed than ever.

"Yes," I answered. "Did you speak, Mr. Crane?"

"No," said Gilbert, "I have nothing to say on the subject." And turning abruptly, he left us and walked rapidly across the lawn and out of the front gate.

"I don't understand Miss Gardiner's attitude," said Mr. Hunt. "I cannot think she had anything to do with the crime, but I do think she is withholding information of some sort. But I must go now, and I will return this evening. Then, if you please, Mr. King, I would like to discuss matters more at length with you."

Hunt went away, and I paced the veranda slowly, thinking things over.

I went round the house, and seeing the Earl in the billiard-room, I went in through the open French window. His lordship seemed disinclined to talk, but he was courteous enough, and by a little diplomacy I succeeded in drawing him out on the subject that absorbed us all.

"But it's better I should say nothing," he declared. "The truth is I've my own opinion of American detectives, and,—well, never mind—only you may as well give up first as last."

The Earl spoke emphatically, and Tom Whiting, coming into the room just then, heard the remark.

"No," declared Tom, "we'll never give up; not till we find that man who shot Philip, and so clear our Milly."

"Clear Milly!" I exclaimed; "why, who could possibly imagine that that child had done any wrong? She is the sufferer, not the culprit."

"I wish everybody thought so," said Tom, with but slightly concealed meaning."

"Doesn't everybody think so?" inquired the Earl, politely.

"Speak for yourself," said Whiting, in a more bitter voice than I had ever heard from the genial chap.

"I think we must admit it's all a mystery," returned the Earl, in his coldest manner; "and perhaps we must also admit that little Miss Leslie is the greatest mystery of all. It's not surprising if her brain is affected by the shock that she should tell those strange stories of throwing things around the room. But if she is rational and perfectly sane, I think we must all admit her statements are mysterious."

Tom Whiting's honest round face showed despair. He couldn't deny Lord Clarendon's assertions, though it was easily seen that he deeply resented them.

"But she sounded perfectly sane and sensible as she gave her testimony," I said. "Of course Miss Leslie is excitable, but she told a straightforward story, and we have no reason to doubt her word."

I realized as I said this that I was speaking insincerely, for I certainly couldn't help doubting Mildred's statement myself. If she had thrown those things, we couldn't have found them on the table when we all went up there immediately after.

I knew, too, that I spoke as I did, out of sympathy for Whiting, and also out of a general sense of chivalry to the girl.

And yet, after all, was it not more generous to ward her, to assume, as Lord Clarence did, that her mind must be affected?

"I think, Whiting," I said slowly, "that while Mildred's statements are untrue, they are not intentionally so. I think she had in her mind such a strong impulse to throw those heavy things that she really thought she did do it."

"Do you think so?" said the Earl, in a most unconvinced way.

"Look here, Lord Clarendon," I said, rather sharply, "are you making implications or insinuations against Miss Leslie? I had reason to think that you greatly admired her."

"So I do," returned his lordship, promptly, "and I make no implication whatever; I hold that the kindest explanation we can make of her conduct, is to believe that she is not quite in her right mind. And I hold that this should be no offence to the lady herself, or to her relatives."

He looked at Whiting as he said this, and Tom returned his glance. There was not a friendly feeling between the two men, and Tom Whiting was not one to make a pretense of such.

"Nurse Lathrop says that Milly's mind is perfectly all right," he said, doggedly, "and I have no reason to doubt her opinion."

"I don't suppose you care for my advice," said the Earl, seriously; "but don't trust that nurse too far. If I'm any reader of character she is disingenuous and not entirely to be trusted."

"We have seen no reason, Lord Clarendon, to feel any dissatisfaction with Miss Lathrop," said Tom, stiffly; "she is devoted to her patient and is exceedingly skilled in her profession."

"She is an English woman," returned the Earl, seeming not at all offended by Tom's manner.

"And though I have every regard and respect for the women of my country as a class, yet perhaps I understand them better than you do over here. And if you'll believe me, that nurse knows more than she tells, and what she tells isn't true."

"You're making grave accusations, Lord Clarendon," I said, amazed at his speech.

"Not accusations," he returned, lightly; "merely my opinions, based on my experience with English women. But it's also my opinion that you'll never know any more about this mystery than you know now. If you had a good man from Scotland Yard, he'd soon find the criminal for you; but with all due respect to the American nation, they have no detectives worthy of the name."

Tom Whiting turned on his heel and walked away. But though I was incensed at his lordship's speech, he made it with such an air of simply stating a self-evident fact, that I wondered if he mightn't be more than half right.

"You see," he went on calmly, after Whiting had gone, "Miss Leslie's story cannot be true. We must all admit that. Also she knows more than she has told. Also in her delirium, she has babbled of things that she doesn't want told, but which of course are known to Nurse Lathrop. Probably, too, Mr. and Mrs. Whiting know these things, which is why Mr. Whiting is annoyed at me."

"But, Lord Clarendon, just what sort of things do you mean? You don't think that Miss Leslie is implicated in the shooting!"

"I do not,—most emphatically I do not. But I do think that Miss Leslie knows far more than she told at the inquest."

"That leads to all sorts of conjectures," said I, thoughtfully.

"What does?" said a voice from the doorway, and Irene Gardiner walked slowly into the room. She was looking superb in a dinner gown of a thin black material, which, trailing behind her, added to her natural dignity. The soft dusky folds of her bodice threw into relief the marble whiteness of her neck and throat, and she wore a long rope of black beads.

I determined to ask her the question that was burning in my mind. "You rarely wear black, Miss Gardiner," I said, taking the risk of being too personal, "and it suits you so well. Didn't you wear a black spangled gown the night of the dance?"

In spite of my intending to ask this question most diplomatically, I had blurted it out in the least tactful way possible. And Miss Gardiner evidently thought so. She gave me first a cold stare, and then seeming to realize that I had asked the question for a definite reason, she flushed painfully and dropped her eyes.

"No," she said, but her voice trembled, "I wore a rose-colored gown, with no black trimming of any sort."

"And a charming gown it was," said the Earl, with a very evident intention of filling an awkward pause. But Irene was not willing to drop the subject.

"What possible interest can you have in the details of my costume?" she asked, turning to me. She had recovered her poise, and her eyes flashed as she seemed to accuse me of a rudeness.

"None," I replied, with a calmness that equaled her own. "Pardon an idle curiosity."

She gave me a glance that denoted anything but pardon, and turned to the Earl.

"It is chilly, isn't it?" she said; "the autumn will be an early one."

"Shall I close the window? May I get you a wrap?" asked the Earl, solicitously; while I stood by, ignored.

"Here is a wrap for Miss Gardiner," said a low voice, and Nurse Lathrop stepped quietly into the room. She brought a light, gauzy scarf, which she adjusted around Irene's shoulders. "I brought this down," she said, by way of explanation, "because I thought you might need it."

This sounded plausible, but after what the Earl had said, I had a dim suspicion that Miss Lathrop might have been eavesdropping and made the scarf a pretext. I fancy Miss Gardiner thought so, too, for she accepted the wrap with a cold "Thank you," and immediately left the room.

"How is your patient, Miss Lathrop?" I asked.

"I cannot say she is any better, Mr. King. It was cruel to make her go through that ordeal this afternoon. The reaction is very great, and she is weak now and shows much loss of vitality."

"Is she delirious?" asked the Earl, directly.

"She is not delirious; but her mind wanders. She tells many things which of course it would not be right for me to repeat. Still, if I thought…"

"Certainly not," said the Earl, sternly. "The secrets of a sick-room should be inviolable."

"But," I began, "if they throw any light on the mystery…"

"They don't!" the Earl again interrupted; "the ramblings of that sick girl's mind have no foundation of truth, and would only confuse the case instead of clearing it!"

"You know a great deal about it, Lord Clarendon!" said Miss Lathrop, with that annoying smile of hers.

"I know what my common sense tells me. And I advise you, nurse, not to tangle things more deeply by repeating Miss Leslie's irresponsible remarks."

"They're not entirely irresponsible; and if I told all I knew, people might look in a different direction from where they're looking now. And perhaps the high and mightiness of some people might have a sudden fall."

As Miss Lathrop glanced out on the veranda where Irene was walking up and down with Tom Whiting, it was impossible not to believe that her hint referred to Miss Gardiner. But I also realized that Irene had not a very friendly attitude toward the nurse, and that doubtless Miss Lathrop's vague remarks were induced merely by a spirit of petty revenge.

Miss Lathrop was not an attractive woman. She was good-looking, but her spirit of self-importance and her readiness to imagine a slight cast upon her, seemed to imply a character of little sweetness and light.

The Earl of Clarendon as if struck by a sudden thought, said abruptly, "Miss Lathrop, I do not think you could tell us anything of importance. But if you do know positively any facts that bear on the case it is of course your duty to divulge them. Your opinions, however, would be entirely uncalled for."

I couldn't help wondering why the Earl treated Miss Lathrop so brusquely. However, she seemed not so much to resent it as to wish to return it in kind.

"Oh, of course I don't know anything of importance," and she smiled superiorly; "but Miss Leslie did say that she thought the motor-coat and goggles might have disguised a woman as easily as a man."

I was thunderstruck at this, but the Earl took it coolly. "Did she say that?" he asked, "or did you suggest it, and she merely acquiesce?"

The flash of surprise in Miss Lathrop's eyes proved that he had hit upon the truth, though she deigned no reply whatever.

"Moreover," he went on, "if Miss Leslie said that, or even agreed to it, it was with the intent of diverting suspicion from a man."

"You don't really think Miss Leslie knows who the intruder was!" I exclaimed, while Miss Lathrop looked at the Earl in utter astonishment.

"Of course I don't," he replied, "nor shall I think so, until she says so herself."

I knew this only meant that he considered it the part of chivalry not to admit any suspicion of Mildred's veracity and sincerity before Nurse Lathrop; though he had certainly given me to understand, that he very much doubted Milly's whole story.

The nurse went away, and her complacent air gave no sign of annoyance; but I was sure, all the same, that the Earl's straightforward talk had at least stirred her calm self-assurance.

"Don't ever try to get information from that woman," said the Earl to me, confidentially; "she would withhold the truth if it suited her purpose, or she would so distort it that it would only lead you astray. You seem to be somewhat of a detective, Mr. King, and I hope you won't take my advice amiss."

"What makes you think I'm inclined to detective work, Lord Clarendon?"

"Only because you ask questions of everybody, and then go away by yourself to puzzle out the answers."

I was inclined to feel a little chagrined at this brief description of my procedure, but the Earl's smile was friendly, and I concluded not to take exception to his good-natured chafing. So I only said, "Well, help me out whenever you can, won't you?" And then we went away to dress for dinner.

XII: An Interview With Milly

WHEN Mr. Hunt came back that evening he found me with Mr. Maxwell in the study. Although I did not wish to pain the old gentleman with more details than were necessary, yet I wanted him to know as nearly as possible how matters stood; and, too, I wanted the benefit of his sound judgment and good advice.

"Come in, Mr. Hunt, come in," I said to the detective. "Let us three sum up the real evidence we have and see what may be best to do next."

I closed the doors in order that we might feel more free to speak in tones which Mr. Maxwell could hear easily, and then I left it to Mr. Hunt to open the conversation.

"First," said the detective, "I would like to know Mr. Maxwell's opinion of Miss Leslie's testimony."

"I have just been reading the stenographer's report of it," said Mr. Maxwell. "I did not hear it clearly, so I asked permission to read the paper myself. I do not know Miss Leslie very well, but she impresses me as nothing more nor less than a merry, light-hearted, innocent girl. Coquettish, perhaps, but I think the depths of her nature are honest and sincere. Now, we have all agreed that her testimony regarding the inkstand and the bronze paper-weight cannot, in the very nature of things, be true testimony. For ink spilled on a carpet will remain there, and bronze horses cannot get up on a table by themselves. Personally, then, I am forced to the opinion that Miss Leslie's mind is affected—temporarily only, I trust. But surely there is no other explanation for her strange statements. And, granting this, may it not be possible that her whole story of the man in the automobile coat is but a figment of her diseased brain?"

"It is possible," said Mr. Hunt, "but they tell me that Miss Leslie is so clear-headed and rational in her conversation that I find it difficult to disbelieve her story of the intruder."

"Nor do I ask you to," said Mr. Maxwell. "I only want to call your attention to the logical point that such grave discrepancies in one part of her recital might argue doubt in other directions.

"I have a logical mind, but I have none of what is often called the 'detective instinct.' That is why I wish to put this whole affair entirely in the hands of an able detective. And again of a detective's ability I do not consider myself a judge. If you think, Mr. Hunt, that you can take care of it successfully, I have sufficient confidence in you to give you the entire responsibility. Or, should you prefer to call in an assistant or an expert from the city, I am quite willing you should do so."

"I don't want to seem egotistical, Mr. Maxwell," said Mr. Hunt, "but I can't help feeling that Mr. King and I can take care of this thing. Mr. King, though not a professional, tells me he has what you have called the 'detective instinct,' at least, in some degree. And if he will help me, I would prefer his assistance to that of a stranger."

"Then we will leave it that way," said Mr. Maxwell. "I shall be glad to have Mr. King for my guest as long as he will stay, and you may consider yourselves authorized to make such investigations as you see fit.

"I do not presume to advise you, but I want to ask you to take an old man's warning, and be sure of your proofs before you act upon them. Clues are often misleading; evidence may be false. But there are certain kinds of facts that point unmistakably to the truth. Those facts you must discover, and then follow where they lead, irrespective of whom they may implicate, and oblivious to any personal prejudice."

I couldn't help wondering if Mr. Maxwell shared my faint but growing suspicion that either Mr. Crane or Miss Gardiner, or both, knew more about the tragedy than they had yet told. I was sure the old gentleman's conservative habits of speech would not allow him to put this into words, but that his sense of justice demanded an intimation of the idea.

After a little further conversation with Mr. Maxwell, we left the study, and Hunt and I went for a walk.

"It's clear to my mind," said Hunt, "that this shooting was done by an intruder from outside, not a common burglar but some past acquaintance of Philip's who had some strong motive for ending the boy's existence.

"It was someone whom Philip knew and recognized. The motive he did not know, for he was both surprised and grieved that this individual should intend to kill him."

"Then you believe Mildred's story, as a whole?"

"Yes. It seems to me that we have as yet no real reason to doubt her main statement, even though the details are mystifying."

"Mystifying! They are impossible!"

"Nothing is impossible in detective work," said Mr. Hunt, "at least nothing that is mysterious."

With that we parted. Mr. Hunt went home, and I went back to Maxwell Chimneys to toss all night on a bed of wakefulness. I felt flattered that Mr. Hunt had asked me to work with him and I resolved to do something that would prove my worth as his assistant.

I thought over what the nurse had said, but dismissed it from my mind as being merely the vagary of an ill-tempered and self-centered nature. I frankly admitted to myself that had her insinuations been directed toward anyone except Irene, I might have given them a little more thoughtful consideration.

But it was out of the question to imagine Miss Gardiner in any way involved in the affair.

And then I thought, suddenly, how I had left her at her own request on the upper veranda, before I saw Philip and Mildred in the library. But I had left her far around on the other side of the house, and later when I returned to tell her of the tragedy, she was on the veranda at the front of house.

To be sure, when I found her there she was crying, or had been. But all these facts gave me no suggestion of her connection with the tragedy, but rather made me anxious to keep my knowledge of her movements to myself, lest anyone else might put on them a wrong construction.

Then I thought about what the Earl had said regarding Mildred's statements. Of course, Mildred Leslie was a frivolous-minded, mischievous girl, and more than once I had known her to make up stories out of her own fanciful brain, entirely for the purpose of astonishing her hearers. But I couldn't think she would do this, when giving witness before a jury. And yet, I well-remembered, when I dashed into the library that night after Crane's fearful announcement, that I distinctly saw the inkstand in the middle of the table.

It was one of those enormous glass and silver affairs, intended as an expensive gift and not always well adapted to practical use. It was, of course, shining and clean, and it was an absolute impossibility, if Mildred had thrown it, that she or anyone else could have replaced it in that immaculate condition in so short a time.

I mulled over the inkstand question until I felt as if my own brains were addled, and I finally fell asleep resolving to make the solution of that puzzle my definite work for the next day.

As a beginning, I begged Dr. Sheldon to allow me a short interview with Mildred the next morning. He hesitated about this, and expressed himself as doubtful of its wisdom. He said his patient was rapidly recovering from the shock sustained by her nervous system, and was now suffering mainly from the flesh wound in her shoulder, but still, he feared that any excitement might bring on fever.

"But, Doctor Sheldon," I said, "I particularly want to avoid excitement. I only want to ask her a few calm and straightforward questions. The nurse and Mrs. Whiting and yourself may all be present, and if you fear that I am alarming or over exciting your patient, I will go away at once."

It required some further persuasion, but at last Doctor Sheldon reluctantly consented to the interview.

I stepped into the sick room, trying to assume a most casual air; and sitting by the girl's bedside, I said, lightly, "I just ran in for a moment to say good morning, and to hope that you will soon be out among us again, for we miss you awfully."

Mildred Leslie may have been ill, and may have been weakened by the shock and by the wound in her shoulder, but to look at her, one would never think it. Two long braids of golden hair lay outside the coverlet, tied at the top by enormous pink bows at each side of her head. The lacy frills of her gown fell away from her baby-like throat, and the piquant face with its dancing blue eyes was as saucy as ever.

One arm of course was in bandages, daintily hidden by the light folds of a lace scarf, but the other hand was held out to me in welcome.

"I'm awfully glad to see you, Mr. King," she said, smiling; "they won't let me see anybody; and going downstairs yesterday afternoon was so perfectly horrid, that I think I ought to see somebody nice to make up for it."

I looked at the girl in secret amazement. How could she show such lightness and gayety after the fearful tragedy she had been through, and which was even yet with us? I felt sure she had never loved Philip, but even so, his dreadful death which had appalled everybody else, must surely have affected her to some degree.

I think Edith Whiting read my thoughts, for she spoke quickly; "I'm glad you've come, too, Mr. King, to cheer Milly up. We do everything we can to keep her mind on pleasant things and away from any trouble."

It seemed to me they had succeeded in their attempts, for certainly Milly's manner was gay and care—free enough, although a little petulant at being kept in her room.

"I could just as well go downstairs as not," she declared, pouting; "you'd carry me down, wouldn't you, Mr. King? I've one good arm that I could put round your neck."

She waved a pretty dimpled arm toward me, and then, taking her hand, as if that would help to pin down her butterfly mind to seriousness for one moment, I spoke to her quietly but decidedly.

"I will carry you downstairs, when the doctor allows it; but just now, Miss Leslie, I want to ask you one or two questions, and I know you'll be kind enough to answer them. I'm sorry that I must turn your thoughts back to a scene that you must naturally try to forget. But please tell me if you are sure that you really threw that inkstand? Might you not have intended to throw it without doing so?"

She looked at me in amazement.

"Certainly I'm sure I threw it," she said. "I distinctly remember picking it up and throwing it at the man. It did not hit him; it fell short of him, for it was heavier than I thought. So then I threw the bronze horse at him. That was heavy, too, and it struck the thick rug with a soft thud. That didn't hit him, either; I never could throw things very well. But I scarcely knew what I was doing, and my acts were impulsive, almost unconscious."

"That is just the point, Miss Leslie; since they were almost unconscious, might it not be that they were not acts at all, merely intention and imagination?"

"I am perfectly sure that I threw those things. Will you tell me why you doubt it?"

"Because," I said, watching her carefully, "when I entered the room where you lay unconscious, the inkstand was undisturbed on the desk, and the bronze horse also."

She drew her hand away from mine, and, as far as it was possible, her pretty baby face assumed a look of hurt dignity.

"I think," she said, "I have as much reason to doubt your statements as you have to doubt mine. For I know I threw those things. The whole affair is like a dream, a vivid dream, in one way; yet in another way every instant of it is more acutely real to me than any other moment of my life.

"I positively threw those things just as I have described to you, and if, which seems impossible, they were returned to the desk, it was done by other hands than mine, either human or supernatural."

The last words were uttered in a rising key and ended in an almost hysterical shriek. She threw her right arm across her eyes, and turning away from me, thereby greatly disturbing her bandaged left shoulder, she burst into a fit of sobbing.

"I told you so!" exclaimed Nurse Lathrop, who had stood during our conversation, with an air of disapproval on her face. She rushed to Milly, almost pushing me out of her way, and as I had promised to do in case this happened, I quickly left the room.

"Oh, Mr. King," exclaimed Edith Whiting, who had followed me, "I'm so sorry you stirred Milly up so! Now she will have brain fever, I know! I daren't go back there, for I am too much upset myself, and the doctor and nurse can take care of her best. But won't you promise me that she shall not be disturbed again?"

It was plain enough that Mrs. Whiting did not blame me, for she knew that the inquiry and investigation must go on. But she seemed to think that I could prevent the further disturbing of her sister.

"I will promise you, Mrs. Whiting," I returned, "that Miss Leslie shall not be questioned again until she is entirely well. I don't think she will have brain fever,—though she will doubtless bring on feverish conditions by that hysterical sobbing."

But even as I spoke Milly's sobs died away and there was silence in the sick room.

In a moment the nurse came out into the hall, and said dictatorially, "You people must go away from here. We have given Miss Leslie an opiate, and I shall not allow any talking, or any noise near this room. It is too bad, Mr. King, that you should have brought on this relapse."

"I'm not willing to take an individual responsibility for it, Miss Lathrop," I returned; "I went to Miss Leslie's room this morning with Doctor Sheldon's full consent."

"Yes! a consent forced from him, and which he knew was most injudicious! And now will you please go away?"

Without another word I bowed and turned away, and Mrs. Whiting went with me. We went down stairs, and finding the music-room empty, she drew me in there.

"You mustn't think Milly heartless," she said, and a sad look came over her face. "But, you see, Doctor Sheldon told us that we must not let her mind dwell on the scene of that night, or it would greatly retard her recovery. So we have not mentioned it, but have tried our best to talk of other things, and to keep her thoughts on joyful and pleasant subjects. We have read to her amusing stories, and Nurse Lathrop has been most ingenious in entertaining her. Don't think hard of us for this, for my little sister is my beloved charge, and I would do anything to help her to a quick recovery."

"I quite appreciate the situation, Mrs. Whiting, and I cannot tell you how sorry I am that it was necessary to have that interview this morning, for it was necessary, for we must continue our investigation; and I had to know whether Miss Leslie's statements were true, or whether at the inquest she was under some sort of hallucination, and detailed imaginary deeds."

"And do you feel sure now that my sister has told you the truth?"

"I must admit the way that she talked to me just now was very convincing. She seemed so entirely herself and so sure of her memory, that I feel I have no reasonable grounds to doubt her assertions."

"And you must not doubt them," said Edith Whiting, earnestly; "I'm sure Milly told you the truth, and I think you will find that out for yourself sooner or later. Will you tell me, Mr. King, why you have—why anybody has a suspicious attitude toward my sister? It seems to me that Milly is one to be avenged, almost as much as Philip. Whoever murdered him, attempted to murder her. Why, then, is his a sainted memory, and my sister talked about and looked at with doubt and uncertainty?"

"Since you ask, Mrs. Whiting, I will admit frankly that there is as yet a mystery about it all. I'd rather not discuss it with you, but, as you know, Miss Leslie is of a volatile, even erratic nature, and ..."

"I know what you're going to say," said Edith sadly; "that as Milly was found with a pistol in her hand, there is a doubt as to the truth of any of her stories! No, don't interrupt me, Mr. King,— I quite understand; and I want you to go ahead with your investigations, and find the murderer as soon as you can. It will not prove to be my sister! But the only way she can be vindicated, is to bring the real criminal to justice and prove the truth of her stories: I don't care if you did see that inkstand on the table, I am perfectly positive, after what she said this morning, that she did throw it at the man who came in at the window, exactly as she says she did! And you will yet believe this, too!"

She went away then, but she had left me something to think about; and she had made me more than ever determined to solve the mystery of the inkstand and the bronze horse before going any further.

XIII: The Mysterious Missiles

I WENT in search of some of the servants and learned from them two important facts: first, that the library had not been swept since Monday night, although it had been dusted; second, that the maid who dusted it distinctly remembered seeing the bronze paper-weight in its usual place, and also asserted that the large inkstand was undisturbed, and that it did not need refilling.

With this new knowledge, or, rather, with this corroboration of previously attested statements, I went to the library, determined to discover something, if I had to remain there all day.

First I looked at the bronze horse as it stood in its place on the library table. This table, which was really a flat-topped desk, was covered with books, writing implements and bric-a-brac of various kinds.

The bronze horse was one of a half dozen different paper-weights, and was a beautiful specimen of its kind. I picked it up and gazed at it intently, wishing it could speak for itself and solve the mystery. As I stared at it I suddenly noticed that one ear was broken off. It was a very small bit that was missing; indeed, scarcely enough to impair the beauty or value of the ornament; but if that missing ear could be found on the library floor, it would be a pretty fair proof that Mildred had thrown the horse in the way she had described.

Eagerly I went in search of the maid whose duty it was to dust the library. In response to my questions she told me that the horse had belonged to Mr. Philip; that it was one of his favorite possessions; and that it was comparatively new. She had noticed the day before that the horse's ear was broken. She could not say positively, but she thought that if it had been broken before that, she would have known it.

Excited at the prospect of something like a real clue at last, I returned to the library and began a systematic search for the missing ear. Getting down on my hands and knees in the space between the desk and the window, I searched, inch by inch, the thick Persian rug and was finally rewarded by discovering the tiny piece of bronze that I was hunting for.

Comparing it with the other ear—indeed, fitting it to the very place from which it was broken—I saw there was no doubt that I had succeeded; and though I could not imagine how the horse had been replaced on the table, I could no longer doubt the truth of Mildred's assertion regarding it.

Carefully wrapping the broken ear in a bit of tissue paper, I put it away and devoted my attention to the inkstand.

The large and elaborate affair stood in the center of the table. The inkwell itself was of heavy cut glass, and was mounted on an ornate silver standard which was also a pen-rack.

The longer I looked at it the more I felt convinced that nobody could disturb the ponderous ornament and restore it again to its place in the way Mildred told of. For it held as much as a small cupful of jet black ink, and even though the Persian rug was of an intricate design in small figures, yet it was light enough in its general coloring to make ink spots perceptible.

Helpless in the face of this assurance, my eye wandered aimlessly over the articles on the desk, when toward the right-hand end and not far from the bronze horse I spied a second inkstand. It was heavy, but not so large as the other, and had no silver standard. I opened it and looked in, and found it to be nearly half-full of red ink.

I looked again at the rug. The predominating color was red in varying shades. Instantly the thought struck me that if Mildred had thrown that inkstand and if there had not been much ink in it, the drops on the carpet would be unobservable because of the similarity of color.

Without stopping to inquire how it could be restored intact to its place, I dropped again to my knees, and again searched for traces. The pattern of the rug being so complicated and mosaic-like, it was almost impossible to discover red spots other than those which belonged there; but at last, I thought I did find on a small white figure red blotches that were not of the Persian dye.

Almost trembling with excitement, I procured from a drawer in the desk a fresh white blotter.

Moistening this, I placed it on the doubtful red spots and gently pressed it. Then lifting it, I found that it showed dull red blurs which had every appearance of being red ink.

Reserving further experiments of this nature to be done in the presence of witnesses, I went in search of Mr. Hunt. He had not yet arrived, so I telephoned him to come as soon as he could. Meanwhile, I returned to the library to think over my discoveries.

I admitted to myself that they gave us no enlightenment whatever, but they had proved the truth of the only doubtful parts of Mildred's story, and left us therefore no excuse for not believing her entire statement.

Hunt soon arrived, and was more than pleased at what I had done.

"I knew you had ingenuity," he said, in his honest, generous way. "Now, I don't believe I should ever have thought of that blotting-paper scheme."

"But what good does it do?" said I.

"Granting that she did throw them, how did they get back to the table?"

"That is another part of the problem," said Hunt, "and one which we need not consider at this moment. First, I think, if you have any more of those clean white blotters, we'll find out the route traveled by that inkstand."

I found plenty of blotters in the drawer, and, proceeding with great care, we succeeded in getting a blotting-paper impression of many more red-ink spots.

We proved to Mr. Hunt's satisfaction, and to mine, that the inkstand had reached the floor about midway between the desk and the window, and that it had then rolled toward the couch, and had stopped just under the long upholstery fringe which decorated the edge of the couch, and which reached to the floor.

"That gives a ray of light!" exclaimed Hunt, triumphantly.

"What do you mean by that?" said I wondering, for I could see no indication of light.

"I can't tell you now," said Hunt, "for someone is coming. I think, Mr. King, it will be wiser to keep these discoveries quiet for the present. Indeed, it is imperative that we should do so."

And so, though I wanted to go at once, and tell Mrs. Whiting that I had proved her sister's statements true, as she had said I would, I restrained myself because of Hunt's advice.

It was Thursday morning when one of the servants told me that Mr. Hunt wanted to see me in the library. I went there at once, and found the detective in conversation with a pretty and very much flustered Swedish parlor-maid.

"This is Emily," said Hunt, in a quiet voice, "she has been telling me of something in which you will be interested. Emily, repeat your story to Mr. King."

The girl fingered her apron nervously as she stood before us, and spoke with embarrassment and hesitation.

"It was this way, yes. I have, the day after the,—the dying of Mr. Philip,—I have to dust in this room. I sweep not, but I do the dusting. And under a chair, yes, under that great soft chair with the fringes I,—I find the jewel,—yes. And I,—oh, it is that I cannot confess!"

The girl buried her face in her apron and seemed unable to go on.

"There, there, Emily," said Hunt, gently, "you kept the jewel and said nothing about it until now. But let that go; we will forgive your stealing the jewel,—now that you have confessed,—if you will tell truly everything you know about it. This is the jewel, King."

He placed in my hand a large topaz set as a seal. It was not a ring, but seemed to me to be a pendant of a watch fob.

"It's part of a fob," said Hunt, "and I want you to look at the design."

The design, deeply cut into the stone, was a crest, coat-of-arms and motto, that I realized at once belonged to the House of Clarendon. Without a doubt it was the property of our noble visitor.

"It's the Earl's," I said simply, as I handed it back to Hunt.

"Yes, of course. And now, Emily, tell Mr. King where you found it."

Reassured by the forgiveness of her theft, the maid showed us where she had found the seal, beneath a chair near the library window. Heavy fringe hung to the floor from the upholstery, and the seal, the girl explained, she had found just inside the fringe, on the rug.

"So," she said, "I have move the chair when I dust him, and I see the sparkle stone, -- yes! I pick him up, and wickedly I put him in my pocket! It is bad, yes; but I'm tempted, and I fall! but you for give? you say so!"

I took little interest in the maid's somewhat dramatic recital, for I was intent on learning just when she had found this thing. It seemed she had found it early Wednesday morning, before I myself had looked for clues, and had found the black spangles. Since she had dusted but not swept, she had not noticed the spangles; but the seal had naturally attracted her attention as being valuable, and she had dishonestly kept it.

"Hunt," I said, "there is one thing I can swear to, and that is --"

"Wait a moment," said Hunt, giving me a warning glance. "I think that is all, Emily; you may go now, and understand, you are forgiven for this theft, only on condition that you tell nobody a single word about the matter."

"Ah, that am I only too glad to do, yes! I do not want that any one should know my baseness! I thank you much, sir, for your goodness, and never, never will I tell."

She left the room and Hunt closed the door.

"It may not mean anything, after all," he said, "for Lord Clarence may have dropped that thing in the library at any time during the day, on Monday. It doesn't implicate him in any way, but I wanted you to hear the girl's story."

"You're wrong, Hunt, it does implicate our noble friend! As I began to say, I can swear that Lord Clarence was wearing that fob himself, at about nine o'clock Monday evening."

"Great goodness!" exclaimed Hunt; "do you really mean that? How do you know?"

"Because he showed it to me, especially. We were in Mr. Maxwell's study,——I remember the people were just beginning to arrive for the dance. We happened to be speaking of seals, and Lord Clarence showed us this one, as a specially fine example of gem engraving. So, my lord was in this room that evening!"

"But it might have been before the murder, King. He might have come in here, casually, as others did, before Philip and Miss Leslie were here."

"But he said at the inquest he wasn't in this room all the evening. And, you know, he didn't come up here when we rushed up. He stayed below, and looked after the guests. I thought that was a particularly clever thing for him to do. But now…"

"And also his lordship has about half an hour on the west veranda unaccounted for, just at the time of the murder. Don't you remember, he said he was smoking a cigarette, and a long gray motor whizzed past him,—and all that. It looks a little queer, King."

"It looks more than a little queer, Hunt. But I can't help thinking there's some commonplace explanation for it, after all."

"How can there be a commonplace explanation? The man had that seal on, you say, at nine o'clock. He says he was not in the library that evening at all. Next morning early, Emily finds the seal here! What's the explanation?"

"I don't know, I'm sure; but what I say is, let's put it right up to him. I know if anybody found evidence against me, I'd rather they'd come straight to me with it, than to go nosing around. And I think that Clarence Personage is a good deal of a man."

"You know I never did share your great admiration of him."

"It isn't a great admiration; but I think he's a right good sort. And I think the fairest way, is to take this seal to him, tell him where it was found, and give him a chance to speak up for himself."

"I'm not sure that's the best plan," said Hunt, doubtfully; "but you know him better than I do, so I'll agree."

Hunt put the seal in his pocket and we went downstairs in search of Clarendon.

It was now nearly noon, and Philip's funeral was to be held that afternoon at two. Even as we went through the hall, quiet-mannered men in black were unfolding chairs and placing them in rows.

The oppressive scent of massed flowers was everywhere, and it seemed incongruous and inappropriate to pursue our errand in this sorrowful atmosphere.

In the study we found Alexander Maxwell and Miss Miranda. The brother and sister were much together, and oftenest in the study, seeming to prefer to be alone there in their grief. Miss Maxwell looked up as we entered, but, as often happened, Mr. Maxwell did not hear us, and so did not turn his head. Not wanting to intrude, I said, quietly, "We're looking for Lord Clarendon. Do you know where he is?"

"He has gone," said Miss Maxwell.

"Lord Clarendon gone! where?" I cried, unintentionally raising my voice in my surprise; and then her brother turned and saw us.

"He has gone home," said Mr. Maxwell; "he remembered an important engagement that called him to the city, and after explaining to my sister and myself that he must go at once, he went, leaving his adieux for the rest of you."

XIV: In Pursuit of the Earl

HERE was a fine state of affairs, indeed! The Earl, whom we wanted so much to see, was gone; and it seemed to me, and I was sure Hunt felt the same, that his going was, in a way, suspicious.

"Why did he go so suddenly?" I asked.

"He had to," returned Miss Maxwell; "he didn't say definitely what his engagement was, but he said it was important."

"I have an idea," said Mr. Maxwell, "that he didn't care to stay for the funeral. You know how queer Englishmen are that way, and I dare say it got on his nerves."

"Nerves nothing!" I exclaimed; "that man is mixed up in the shooting of Philip, and now we've let him get away! Hunt, tell Mr. Maxwell the circumstances."

So the detective told the two interested listeners about the finding of the letter and the conclusions we must draw from it.

"You see," I said, "I know, and you do too, Mr. Maxwell, that the Earl was in this room wearing that seal at about nine o'clock Monday evening. Early next morning it was found in the library. The Earl denied having been in the library at all that night, and so, you must admit, an explanation is called for."

"But I can't think that the explanation would prove Lord Clarendon guilty of the crime,—or even accessory," said Mr. Maxwell, looking thoughtfully at the gem he held in his hand; "he had no quarrel with our boy."

"He greatly admired Miss Leslie," I said, knowing it to be the truth.

"But he had only known her a day or two," broke in Miss Miranda's gentle voice; "he couldn't possibly become so infatuated in that short time that he would commit a crime for her! And besides, he's a nobleman."

The good lady had always been deeply impressed by the glory of the Earl's title,—a truly American weakness; and she could think no ill of one who rightfully displayed a coronet. But to my mind the fact of his being a foreigner, and a titled one at that, rather argued against him; though I realized that my prejudice was quite as illogical as Miss Maxwell's.

"Aside from any possible motive," said Hunt, "we have to explain the discrepancy between the Earl's statement that he was not in the room and the finding of a piece of his personal property there. You returned the fob to him after looking at it, I suppose?"

"Certainly I did," said Mr. Maxwell, a little shortly; "but I cannot agree that the finding of it in the library implicates his lordship in our tragedy."

"What then would be your hypothesis, sir," said Hunt, "as to finding it in the library?"

"My hypothesis, Mr. Hunt, would be, that the maid, Emily, did not tell the truth, rather than that the Earl of Clarendon did not."

"I hadn't thought of that," I said; "to be sure, that girl might have made up the story, but I can't see why she should do so. She would have kept the jewel, but that Mr. Hunt in questioning her about her dusting of the library, surprised her into a confession. She is simple-minded and emotional, and her confession, I am sure, was entirely truthful."

"It may be," said Mr. Maxwell, coldly; "but I cannot think that logically you have any more reason to assume truthfulness on her part than on the part of the Earl."

"Emily might have found it somewhere else," suggested Miss Maxwell.

"Then why make up that story?" said Hunt.

"I don't know, I'm sure, unless to make a sensation. She's a queer girl and I've never understood her."

"I'm positive that she did not make up that story, dear Miss Maxwell," said I; "and I know if you had heard her, you would agree with me. But I am willing to admit that there may be and probably is some commonplace explanation; and whatever it may be, we must know it before we go any further. Do you know where the Earl has gone?"

"Yes," said Miss Maxwell, "he went to New York. I think he is staying at the Waldorf; at least, that's where he was just before he came to us."

"Then I'm going straight there to see him," I declared, "and I shall start at once."

Hunt looked his approval of this, but the other two did not.

"I don't think you'd better, King," said Mr. Maxwell, slowly; but Miss Maxwell grasped my arm impulsively, and said, "Oh, don't go, Peter! please don't go until after the funeral, anyway."

I couldn't resist her pathetic appeal, and I agreed not to go until after the funeral, but I insisted on my plan of going then.

"Did the Earl say good-by to Miss Leslie?" I asked Miss Maxwell, pausing, as I was about to leave the room.

"Oh, no," she answered; "Milly is very ill again. The excitement of that talk with you this morning threw her into a high fever and we are all very anxious about her. I told Lord Clarendon this, and it was after that, that he told me he was going."

"Because of it?" asked Hunt, suddenly.

"No, of course not. In fact he left a message for Milly in addition to his good-by, to the effect that she would be glad he had gone."

"What could he have meant by that, Miss Maxwell?"

"I don't know, unless he felt that his attentions to her had been unwelcome, and she would be glad to know he was gone."

"No man's attentions are unwelcome to Mildred Leslie," I said, "and I don't think that's what he meant at all. I tell you, Miss Maxwell, that man is mixed up in our trouble, and Milly Leslie knows it. Suppose for a moment that it was the Earl who shot Philip, wouldn't Philip exclaim, 'Oh, to think he should shoot me!' and wouldn't Milly, if she knew or suspected it, be glad to have the Earl go away?"

"Peter," said Mr. Maxwell, somewhat sternly, "your suggestion is monstrous! I should be angry at you, were it not that your idea is so absurd! You are carried away with your desire to detect somebody or something. Now, my boy, put this all out of your mind, at least for the present. This afternoon we shall give the last honors we can to our Philip; and after that it will be time to turn our attention to avenging the crime that took him from us."

Mr. Maxwell's manner was impressive, and I felt rebuked that I should have obtruded my theories and suspicions at this moment. I said as much, in an apologetic way, and then Hunt and I withdrew.

"You're dead right, Mr. King," said Hunt, after we had left the study; "it was his Noble Nibs that turned the trick! And I hope you will track him down at once. You can take that five o'clock train to New York, but, even so, he has hours the start of you. I wish the old people would let you go now."

"No, I can't offend those gentle souls by insisting on that. But I'll go up this afternoon, Hunt, and I'll find that man, unless he has really fled from justice."

I don't care to dwell upon the sad rites of that afternoon. It was hard to realize that we were gathered there to pay the last honors to Philip Maxwell. He had always been so alert and alive, so light-hearted and debonair, that it was difficult to think of him as dead. And the mystery of his death added a peculiar horror to it all.

But at last the ceremonies were over, and I was free to go away if I chose. I hesitated about discussing the matter again with the Maxwells, for I knew they would oppose my going to New York on such an errand. And though I might persuade them that it was my duty to do so, the argument would doubtless be a long one, and I might be late for the train I wanted to take.

So I asked Hunt to tell them that I had gone, and to say that I would soon return. I advised him, too, to tell them that it was the most straight forward thing to do. For, if the Earl could give a simple and rational explanation of the question of the seal, certainly no harm would be done. And if he could not, surely the matter must be looked into.

And so I found myself in the train, returning over the road that Miss Gardiner and I had traveled a few days before.

Naturally my thoughts strayed to her, for mysterious though she was in some ways, she had made a greater impression on my heart than ever woman had done before. I ascribed her strange ways to her strength of character, and her cold logic to her high order of intellect. If a thought crept in that she knew more than she had told about the mystery, I determinedly put it away from me.

It seemed to me everybody was acting mysteriously. Mildred Leslie was inexplicable. Her rapid transitions from gay thoughtlessness to feverish hysterics surely denoted guilty knowledge of some sort. Miss Lathrop was queer enough, too; but of course, she could know nothing about the crime, except what she had heard from us, or what Mildred had revealed in her delirium.

Irene was strange; Gilbert Crane had acted very strangely, and certainly Lord Clarence's behavior was astonishing.

However, I didn't really think the nobleman had done the shooting; but I did think that he knew something about it that he preferred not to tell, and so had put himself beyond questioning.

Before ten o'clock I was at the Waldorf, inquiring for the Earl, only to be informed that he was out. He had left no word of his whereabouts at the office, but as he still retained his rooms I decided to wait for him. The clerk told me that he had come to the hotel that afternoon about four, and later had gone out, apparently to dinner.

But though I waited until midnight, his lordship did not appear.

Again I conferred with the clerk, telling him I was especially anxious to see the Earl of Clarendon. He was not greatly disturbed over my anxiety, but was willing to do what he could, and suggested that I interview his lordship's man-servant. This was a truly brilliant idea, and I directed that the valet be sent for. But the response was, that Lord Clarendon's man,—by name, Hoskins,— was not at present in the hotel.

"Did he go away with the Earl?" I inquired, but this, nobody seemed to know.

The Earl had left at about six o'clock, and as it was now twelve, all the porters and bell-boys had shifted, and no one at present on duty could give me the information I wanted. Nonplussed, I told the clerk that I would go to his lordship's rooms and wait for him there; for secretly I had a hope that I might learn something from an examination of his apartments. But permission to do this was refused me; and then, though I didn't want to hint my suspicions openly, I gave the clerk to understand, that it was in the character of a detective that I wished to see the Earl's rooms. Whereupon the clerk nonchalantly asked to see my badge. As I had none, not being a real detective at all, he seemed to consider the interview closed; and realizing I could do nothing more that night, I asked for a room and went to bed.

I rose the next morning with a firm determination to find the Earl. Surely such a personage could not drop out of civilization without leaving a trace; and he had kept his apartments at the hotel, so he evidently intended to return. But to sit and wait for him was not my plan. I went downstairs and inquired for him at the desk, but, as I had anticipated, I received no information whatever, except that he was not at present in the hotel. I thought it over, as I ate breakfast on the sunny side of the dining-room, and at last a brilliant idea came to me. I was determined to do real detective work in this matter; something more than merely making inquiries of a secretive clerk.

My brilliant plan might not prove successful, but after breakfast I put it at once to the test. Going up in the elevator, I stepped off at the fourth floor where the Earl's rooms were, instead of going on to my own on the ninth floor. I knew the Earl's apartment was numbered four ninety-two. I managed to get to its door unobserved, and then stood there, hesitating, as if just leaving the room.

I stood thus for some time, but my patience was finally rewarded by seeing a chamber-maid coming along the hall.

"Ah! there you are," I said, stepping briskly forward; "Now, look here, my good woman, I find that I put an important paper in my waste-basket by mistake. When did you empty the baskets?"

"Last evening, sir," she said, looking a little alarmed. "It should have been done earlier, sir, but I got behind-hand with my work, and -- "

"Never mind; show me the place where the papers were thrown. They're not burned yet, are they?"

She hesitated, but a powerful argument that was green and crisp induced further information.

"They're in a sack, in my broom-closet, sir. But I'd be fined if it were known..."

"It sha'n't be known, I promise you. There's no one about; show me where they are. I want to see the contents of the basket that was in four ninety-two."

"They're all together, sir, but that room is near the top. Step in here, please."

I followed the woman into her broom-closet, which proved to be a small but fairly well lighted room. She took up a large sack and tossed part of its contents out on the floor.

"Will you search, yourself, sir? I must be at my work."

"Yes, my good woman, go along. I'll find what I want, and no one will be the wiser."

She went away and I began the well-nigh hopeless task of looking over the waste paper. But after a time I began to find torn envelopes addressed to the Earl of Clarendon, and these I examined with interest. There were many invitations, advertisements and personal letters, but none seemed to bear on his present absence until I struck a note from one Mrs. Ogilby Pauncefote. This was an invitation to her country house on Long Island, at Osprey-by-the-Sea. The lady asked Lord Clarendon to come the afternoon before, and as I found also a time table with the railroad station checked, I couldn't help thinking that his lordship had accepted her invitation.

At any rate I found nothing else to give me any idea of where the nobleman had gone, and I resolved to go to this place, and if he were not there, perhaps to learn from Mrs. Pauncefote where he might be. Making use of the discarded time-table, I started at once toward my destination.

But taking the first available train, it was eleven o'clock when I reached the ornate mansion at Osprey-by-the-Sea.

The footman who answered my ring informed me that Mrs. Pauncefote was not at home.

"Is the Earl of Clarendon here?" I inquired.

"No sir; he has been here all night, but he went with the party in the yacht."

"Ah, in the yacht," I said, endeavoring to assume an air of intimacy with the family. "What time did they start?"

"At ten o'clock, sir."

I looked at my watch. "Then they've been gone about an hour," I observed.

"And where are they headed for?"

"Montauk Point, sir."

"Montauk Point! why they can't reach that till late this afternoon."

"No, sir; they will lunch on board the yacht, and reach the point by dinner-time,—or I should say, perhaps at tea-time, about four o'clock, sir."

He was an amiable sort of man, and as he probably thought me a friend of the family, he was giving me all the information he could.

"H'm," I said; "I wonder how I could catch up to them. Could I get a motor-boat anywhere?"

"I don't think you could overtake the Butterfly that way, sir. She's a clipper. But of course you could take the train."

This seemed to be the only thing to do, and I turned away and went back to the railway station. If I had only risen earlier and started sooner, I could have found my Lord Clarence with no trouble at all. But there was nothing for it but to keep on to Montauk Point. I had time before my train went, to send a telegram to Hunt, in which I told him that I was making progress and was on the trail of the Earl.

XV: The Earl's Story

I GREW very impatient during the long ride. I had no appetite for luncheon, and occupied myself with wondering whether I were not on a wild goose chase. The yacht, *Butterfly*, might change her course and I might wait in vain on the eastern end of Long Island. But surely I was following a direct clue. Surely we wanted the Earl and I was taking the only way to find him. I reached Montauk Point and went at once to the dock where the Pauncefotes' steam-yacht might be expected to arrive. She was not in, so I waited with such patience as I could command and at last she came—a beautiful craft which seemed to be the last word in elaborate luxury.

As the party came ashore I looked in vain for my elusive nobleman, but he was certainly not with them. There were a dozen or more fashionable people, and deciding that the gray-haired, important looking lady was the hostess, I went up to her and introduced myself. With polite apologies for intruding, I inquired for the Earl of Clarendon.

Mrs. Pauncefote was exceedingly affable.

"Why, Mr. King," she said, "we did have Lord Clarence with us, but he had an engagement in New York that made it necessary for him to be there at five o'clock. So we put him off at Wading River and he took the train back to town. We hated awfully to do it, and we really came near kidnapping him and bringing him along with us; but he insisted so that we had to let him go, though it broke our hearts! didn't it, Gerry?"

Miss Geraldine Pauncefote, the daughter of the important lady, agreed that they were indeed desolate at losing the Earl, and she even suggested that I should take his place in their merry party.

"I should only be too glad to do so," I replied, glancing regretfully at the pretty girl, but it is imperative that I find the Earl as soon as possible. Can you tell me if he is going directly to his hotel?"

"I don't know, really," returned Miss Pauncefote; "I was so annoyed at him for deserting us that I wouldn't speak to him when he went away."

"He must indeed have had an important engagement to go in those circumstances," I said, smiling at her; "and I must go away I fear with a similar abruptness. But you'll speak to me, won't you?"

"Yes," she said gaily, "if you'll promise to come with us some other time. We go sailing nearly every day."

"I shall only be too glad to do so. By the way, Miss Pauncefote, may I ask you if Lord Clarence seemed anxious or troubled in any way?"

"Not that exactly," she said, thoughtfully, "but he was quiet and rather sad. He told me that a friend of his had just died, but he gave us no particulars. However, I think that was the real reason he left our merry-making, and not because of an engagement in town."

"And it was most considerate of him," said Mrs. Pauncefote; "for I'm sure there was no reason why my house party should have its pleasure spoiled by the death of somebody we didn't know. And of course, if the Earl felt sad, it was far better for him to go away than to remain, and act gloomy."

This seemed a little heartless, and yet I realized that a hostess does not like an unnecessary cloud to mar the happiness of her party. With a few more words of leave-taking, I went back to the railway station.

I was getting a little tired of railroad travel, but I had no choice save to follow the developments of my case, so I accepted it with as good a grace as possible, and seven o'clock found me back at the Waldorf, once more endeavoring to extract information from the taciturn clerk. Again he disclaimed all knowledge of the Earl or his movements, and with a feeling of utter disappointment, I stood around in the crowded lobby.

I was uncertain just what I should do next, when a cordial voice said, "Well, Mr. King, and how do you do?"

I looked up startled, to see Lord Clarence, himself, holding out his hand. In my gratitude at finding him, I grasped it and shook it warmly, but I did not tell him that I had just traveled the length of Long Island in search of him.

"Have you dined?" he asked; "no? Then dine with me, won't you? I assure you, I'd be glad of your company. Do you know, Mr. King, I can't shake off the horror of that Maxwell affair. I went off with a yachting party, by way of diversion, but it jarred too terribly, and I left the yacht somewhat abruptly, and came back to New York. I've never been through such an experience before, and that death of young Maxwell was an awful thing. Awful!"

I accepted the Earl's invitation and went with him to the dining-room, my mind in a complete chaos. If the Earl were in any way implicated in the mystery, he certainly was putting up a magnificent bluff. And if he were entirely innocent, as he seemed, then I wanted to talk matters over with him.

It was difficult to accuse him, or even to imply his possible connection with the tragedy, in the face of his straightforward and earnest sympathy.

"You stayed for the funeral, I suppose," he observed, after the first course had been served to us; "I couldn't do it. The whole affair got awfully on my nerves. What is your theory of the crime, if I may ask?"

Here was an opening, but I countered. "I'm rather at sea, Lord Clarence," I returned, "what do you think about it all? Often an outsider can get a better perspective than those more closely associated with the occurrence."

The Earl sipped his soup, thoughtfully. "I hesitate to say what I think," he said, slowly, "for I have so little on which to base any opinion. But do you mean to tell me that nothing has been accomplished by the police or the detectives?"

"It isn't really in the hands of the police," I said, a little apologetically; "You see Mr. Maxwell thinks Mr. Hunt can ferret out the truth, and I am trying to help him."

The Earl looked up at me with a flash of amusement in his eyes. "And you're helping him," he said, "by trailing me?"

I was chagrined and not a little embarrassed.

Surely a guilty man could not show that expression of indulgent amusement. Surely no one even indirectly associated with the crime, could wear such an aspect of serious concern and honest inquiry.

I concluded that frankness would be the best plan for me.

"I did come in search of you, Lord Clarendon," I said; "for I wanted to ask your explanation of a certain bit of evidence. And as I think you would prefer it, I will put the matter to you without preamble."

"I should certainly prefer direct accusation to beating about the bush."

"It isn't accusation," I responded, "and it's simply this. This seal, which is doubtless one of your belongings, was found on the floor of the library where Philip Maxwell was shot. It was found there the morning after the murder; and if you remember, you were wearing it, and in fact showing it to us, in Mr. Maxwell's study, on Monday evening before the tragedy."

I laid the seal on the table before him, and the Earl looked at it thoughtfully.

"It certainly looks like a case against me, Mr. King; and I cannot blame you or the detective, Hunt, for thinking that it implicates me very seriously in the crime. Indeed, I think that our Scotland Yard men would think it a fairly strong piece of evidence. Now, Mr. King, I take it you don't accuse me of the murder. Or, do you?"

"Certainly not," I replied; "But I ask you to remember, Lord Clarence, that you stated at the inquest that you had not been in the library that evening at all. So I merely ask you how it came about that this jewel was found there?"

"But, Mr. King, since you don't suspect me of the murder, what is it of which you do accuse me? Complicity or concealed knowledge?"

"Not necessarily complicity, but possibly concealed knowledge. But understand, I do not accuse you; I merely ask the explanation, hoping, and indeed, feeling fairly sure that you can make it."

"That's just the trouble, Mr. King; I can't give you an explanation."

"What, you mean you don't know how the seal came to be there?"

"I don't say that; but I say I cannot give you the explanation."

"Then you practically confess that you are concealing knowledge important for us to know. I think, Lord Clarence, we shall have to insist on that explanation."

"By what authority, Mr. King?"

"In the interests of right and justice."

"That is a strong argument," and the Earl looked thoughtful. "Indeed, I'm not sure but that it is my duty to tell you all I know. Of course, Mr. King, you must know why I hesitate."

"I don't," I returned, flatly.

"Well, of course you must know that I didn't kill Philip Maxwell, and that I had no interest in having him killed. Nor do I want to express any opinion, that may be wrong or unfounded, and thereby cast suspicion toward one who may be,— who must be entirely innocent."

"Meaning whom?" I asked, breathlessly.

"That's just what I hesitate to say. As you well know, a slight bit of ocular evidence goes so far, and is so difficult to suppress, though it may mean nothing."

"Lord Clarence," I said, seriously, "if you will tell me what you know, I will promise that the secret shall be carefully guarded, and put to no use whatever, unless we can feel sure that it will positively lead to the discovery of the criminal."

"Then I will tell you about this seal. As you remember, I was showing it to Mr. Alexander Maxwell in his study, and you were present. That was just before the guests arrived for the dance. Very shortly after, I danced with Miss Leslie. She told me, laughing, that a watch fob was entirely incorrect with evening clothes, and in obedience to her pretty, willful dictate, I took the fob off my watch. She admired this seal, being especially interested in the crest, and I detached it from the rest of the fob and gave it to her."

"As an out and out gift?"

"Yes; I was greatly attracted by Miss Leslie, in fact I quite lost my head over her. She attached the seal to a long neck-chain she was wearing, and seemed childishly delighted with it. She is a strange little person, isn't she?"

"She is. And since you were not in the library that night, it is to be supposed then, that she lost this seal from her chain while she was there with Philip."

"Or perhaps she purposely detached it to throw at the intruder. It is a heavy missile, you know, and the little lady seemed inclined to throw anything she could lay her hands on."

I pondered a few moments on this. The fact that the seal was found under the chair, near the window, lent a probability to the Earl's assumption.

"But why didn't she mention this, when she told her story?" I said.

"Ah, who can understand a woman? Miss Leslie declared she threw things which she couldn't possibly have thrown, and then fails to tell of a missile she could and probably did throw."

"But you don't think Mildred Leslie in any way guilty?" I exclaimed; "and besides, she did throw that horse and inkstand." And then I detailed to the Earl how we had found the red ink stains, and the broken ear of the horse.

He looked utterly astounded. "But," he said, "how could those things get back on the table again?"

"That is the mystery. To me it simply proves that someone else was in that room later who had a reason for wanting those things restored to their places."

"And you thought I did it, and left my seal by mistake," said the Earl, smiling a little; "but Mr. King, to return to your former question, I do not think Miss Leslie guilty of any part in the shooting, but I do think she knows very well who the intruder was."

"You do!" I exclaimed; "why I had never thought of that! Why do you think so?"

"Since you have promised to keep these matters confidential, at your discretion, I will tell you of the motor-car that I saw while I was on the lower veranda. That car, with four men in it, was coming in when I saw it, not going out. That would be about ten minutes after ten. I've been thinking that out. Then as you know, I returned to the dancing-room, of course, giving no further thought then to the car, and at half-past ten Mr. Crane announced to us the news of the tragedy. My theory is, Mr. King, that the murderer came in that car, shot young Maxwell and went away again. I think the whole affair was premeditated and carefully planned by the murderer. And I think, moreover, that Miss Leslie recognized the intruder in spite of his disguise, and is withholding and confusing her evidence through a desire to shield him."

I thought it over. It was all a new theory to me, and though it might not be the true one, it called for investigation. "When you were on the lower veranda, you were on the library side of the house?" I went on.

"Yes; and that car came in swiftly and passed me."

"Going around toward the back of the house?"

"Yes; there is a little staircase that runs from the lower veranda to the upper one."

"Not on the library side?"

"No, on the other side. But of course a man running up that staircase, could easily reach the library window by going around the house on the upper veranda, or by going through the house."

"If he were not intercepted. But a man in full automobile togs could hardly go around or through, unnoticed."

"I'm not explaining the details, I'm only stating a possible theory. And I think there was no one on the upper veranda at that time. We were all in the dancing-room or somewhere on the lower floor."

"Miss Gardiner was up there," I said, thoughtlessly; "I left her there as I came downstairs."

"Then if my theory is the true one, and if the man did go round the verandas and appear at the library windows in accordance with Miss Leslie's story, Miss Gardiner must have seen him."

I quickly dropped the subject of Irene Gardiner, as I did not wish her even tacitly involved in this matter. "Frankly, you do not believe Miss Leslie's story, then?" I said.

"Frankly, I do not," replied the Earl; "and that is the reason I left Maxwell Chimneys when I did. I learned that Miss Leslie had become much worse, and was growing feverish and hysterical, and I honestly thought that my departure would help her to feel more secure and less harassed. I feared it might come about that I should have to tell of this motor-car, and that it would worry or annoy Miss Leslie to think that I had seen it. And it might be the means of disclosing something that she didn't wish to have known. I felt sure she had done something with my seal, because I asked her sister the next day if it were on her chain when she was carried to her room, and Mrs. Whiting told me it was not. Altogether, Mr. King, though perhaps my reasons were not entirely logical, they were sufficiently strong to make me want to leave Maxwell Chimneys."

"To be honest, you had lost your deep interest in Miss Leslie."

"To be honest, I had. She is most attractive, an unusual type to me, and positively fascinating. But I cannot think her entirely truthful; and at any rate, I preferred to come away, lest my presence should disturb her or make harder for her the sorrow she has to bear and the part she has to endure in the tragedy. That is my story, Mr. King, and I assure you that I have no direct suspicion of anybody; and moreover, that I came away myself merely out of consideration for Miss Leslie. I trust you're convinced of my own honesty and truthfulness?"

"I am, indeed," I said, heartily; "I should apologize to you for having come to New York to find you, if I had unjustly suspected you. But I did not do that, Lord Clarendon. We found your seal in suspicious circumstances, and I deemed it only fair to us and to you to give you an opportunity to explain it. You have done so, to my entire satisfaction, and I thank you. Shall I give you back your property, or do you consider that it belongs to Miss Leslie?"

"As I really presented it to her, I don't like to take it back. Suppose you take it to her, Mr. King, and if she doesn't wish to keep it, send it to me again. But if she does, by all means let her have it."

"One thing more, Lord Clarence; since you have put thought on this matter, what in your opinion could be the motive of the man in the car for committing such a crime?"

"Of that I can form no theory. Of course he must have had some grudge against Philip Maxwell, or he must have been a jealous suitor of Miss Leslie's. But I think, Mr. King, your next move should be to discover the identity of that car and its occupants."

"We certainly shall try to do so, Lord Clarence, though I fear we have let too much time pass. It is not easy to trace a car after so many days, and with no knowledge whatever of the men in it."

"No, it will not be easy," said the Earl, "but I am sure that if she would do so, Miss Leslie could give you the information you want. Another thing, Mr. King, since you're kind enough to listen to my suggestions, I think Miss Lathrop, the nurse, knows more than she has told."

"But how can she? You remember she didn't come to the house at all, until after the crime had been committed."

"No; but she has had opportunity to hear Miss Leslie's talk in her delirium. Without a doubt, the girl told many things which the nurse, with her extreme idea of professional ethics, is not willing to reveal. This is merely a suggestion, Mr. King, but if you can find out anything from that nurse, I think it will prove of importance."

Truly the Englishman gave me food for thought. At his request, we dismissed the subject from our dinner conversation; but I had carefully laid up in my memory all he had said, and resolved to act upon it later.

XVI: The Gray Motor-Car

SATURDAY morning I went back to Maxwell Chimneys. Though I had done very little, if anything, toward a definite solution of the mystery, yet I had eliminated the Earl as a possible factor in the case, and surely that was something.

At the luncheon table I told about it, but only in a general way, and without going into details. After luncheon, however, Mr. Hunt arrived, and we had a conference in Mr. Maxwell's study. The guests of the house were all present except Miss Leslie and her nurse.

Mr. Maxwell led the discussion. "I've been thinking it over, Peter," he said, "while you were away, and I've pretty much come to the conclusion that we may as well give up our efforts to find the man who shot Philip. I was sure, before you went away, that the Earl of Clarendon had no hand in it, and I cannot think that we shall ever learn who was in the mysterious motor-car that Lord Clarence saw that night. And should we find the car, I dare say it would turn out to be some tradesman or other equally innocent person. I, myself, am too old to take an active part in any search. Both my sister and I have a prejudice against calling in the police or applying to the detective bureau. And so, it seems to me, that my sister and I would rather bear our grief undisturbed by harrowing publicity."

"I quite appreciate your ideas, Mr. Maxwell," said Tom Whiting, respectfully; "but I want to call to your attention the fact that my wife's sister is, in a way, under a suspicion of knowing who that intruder was, and of being willing to shield him. Now we can't stand for this! Edith and I have agreed that, unless you positively forbid it, we must at least make an attempt to discover who that man was. You see, the Earl of Clarendon thinks that the man in that motor-car came up on the veranda, and shot Philip through the library window. Moreover, he distinctly implies that Milly knows who the man is, and will not tell; and that he, the Earl, went away lest his knowledge of the car and its occupants should annoy or disturb Milly. Now this is all utter poppycock! Milly isn't shielding any man. She doesn't know who that intruder was,—although Philip did. Now, I propose to track that car, and that man, whether he is the criminal or not!"

"Go ahead, Mr. Whiting, if you like," said Hunt; "but you'll find yourself on a wild goose chase. To my mind, that precious Earl is not so innocent as he makes out! He pulled the wool over Mr. King's eyes, but he doesn't fool me. And trying to hide behind a woman's skirts. is just what I should expect from a British rascal of his stamp!"

"Oh, Mr. Hunt," said Miss Miranda, looking greatly pained; "please don't talk like that about one of my guests! Why, he scarcely knew Philip, and he had no reason for wishing him ill."

"He was in love with a girl that Philip was as good as engaged to," said Hunt, bluntly; "that's enough motive for his state of mind toward Philip."

"There it is," said Mr. Maxwell, "as soon as you detectives begin to suspect anybody you let your imagination run away with you. Granting the Earl of Clarendon was attracted by Miss Leslie, it doesn't follow that he would shoot another man who happened to be in love with her, also! No, the Earl is entirely innocent, and the criminal is as far removed from our knowledge or suspicion as he ever was."

"But he won't be," said Tom Whiting, "if I can once catch that motor-car! Can't you all see clearly how a man from that car could have run up that little back staircase, around the veranda, and back again after committing the crime in a very short space of time? Of course he must have been an enemy of Philip's, and of course he must have had his plans carefully laid. But a murderer always lays his plans carefully. He doesn't go around on a casual chance!"

"But if your theory is the right one," observed Hunt, "Miss Gardiner must have seen that man, for she was on the upper veranda at the time of the crime."

"Did you see anybody, Irene?" said Edith Whiting, but she said it perfunctorily, for she knew if Miss Gardiner had seen a stranger she would have told of it before this.

"No, of course not," said Irene; "Do you suppose if I had seen Philip Maxwell's murderer I shouldn't have said so long ago? I think, with Mr. Maxwell, that he can never be found; and I see no use in keeping up a search for that motor-car. I doubt if the Earl saw one anyway."

"Good gracious!" exclaimed Tom Whiting, "why is it that everybody doubts the Earl's veracity? Surely he would have no reason for making up that story of the motor-car! Certainly he saw it; and I, for one, am determined to find out about it!"

"Yes, do," said Mrs. Whiting; "for I can never rest happy until Mildred is entirely cleared from any suspicious thought. The poor child has enough to bear, without the added insult of an unjust suspicion."

"What does she say about the Earl's seal?" I asked.

"We haven't asked her yet," returned Mrs. Whiting. "Nurse Lathrop is to ask her as soon as Milly wakens from her nap."

"Perhaps Milly has wakened already," said Miss Maxwell, and acting on that suggestion, Edith went upstairs to see.

In a few moments the nurse came down, leaving Edith with the patient. The white, stiffly-starched personage came into the room with her usual air of professional importance, and taking a chair, folded her hands primly, awaiting questions. Miss Maxwell spoke gently: "Have you asked Milly, Miss Lathrop, about the seal the Earl gave her?"

"Yes, I have, Miss Maxwell."

"And what did she say?" went on the gentle voice, which was such a contrast to the nurse's cold, metallic tones.

"She said that the Earl gave it to her."

"Did she say she left it in the library? Tell us all she said, can't you?" This was from Mr. Maxwell, who was clearly impatient at the aggravating slowness of Miss Lathrop's story, and indeed he voiced what we all felt.

The nurse rolled her hard eyes slowly toward him. "I would rather be questioned," she said. "I might say more than would be discreet."

"Oh, bother discretion!" exclaimed Tom Whiting, whose nerves were on edge; "the Seal business doesn't amount to anything, anyway; and you're purposely trying to make it seem important."

"Why should I do that?" and Miss Lathrop smoothed her immaculate apron in a most exasperating manner.

"I don't know why you should, and I don't care," went on Whiting. "Here I'll question you. After Milly said the Earl gave her the seal, what did you ask her next?"

"I asked her what she did with it?"

"And what did she say?"

"She said she fastened it on her neck-chain."

"And after that?"

"She said she pulled it off her chain and threw it at the man."

"What man?"

"The man that shot Mr. Maxwell."

"Oh, she did, did she? That's just what I supposed. Did she throw it before she threw the horse or after?"

"I don't know, Mr. Whiting."

"And it doesn't make a scrap of difference anyhow! Mr. Maxwell, there's the whole seal story. The Earl gave it to Milly, and she wore it on a chain. With the impulse, which she has already described, and which is a very natural feminine instinct, to throw something at the intruder, she grabbed that heavy jewel from her chain and threw it. She probably didn't hit him, but whether she did or not, the seal fell under the edge of the chair, and was found next morning by Emily. This in no way implicates his lordship, and you can readily see that he went away, lest he should seem to know anything that might react against Milly, in an ultra-suspicious mind! Now, then, the Earl is out of the question, once for all, to my mind, and the only suspicion we have left, tends toward that motor-car, which must have brought here the man who shot both Philip and my sister. Even though you, Mr. Maxwell, do not wish to trace this man, I hold that I have a right to do so; for the fact that he did not kill Milly, in no way excuses his intent and effort to do so!"

"Do not misunderstand me, Mr. Whiting," said Mr. Maxwell; "as I said, I am unable myself to work actively in the matter. But you must surely know that I'm entirely in sympathy with your feeling, and that I wish as much as you do, to bring the villain to an accounting. If you will instigate and conduct the Search, I will defray any expenses incurred, and thus, in a way, do my share."

"All right, Mr. Maxwell," said Whiting, with enthusiasm.

"I only wanted your sanction to go ahead with my plans, King, I hope you will help me. Mr. Hunt, may I also count on you?"

"Of course," said Hunt, "but I tell you frankly, Mr. Whiting, that I cannot believe, as the rest of you do, in the entire innocence of that English Earl!"

"And I want to say," said Irene Gardiner, "that while I cannot share Mr. Hunt's actual suspicion of the Earl, I do think we ought to verify his story by some evidence other than his own."

"That's just what we're going to do, Irene," said Tom Whiting; "if we spot that car and nail the man we want, that's going to prove the Earl a real detective, and worthy of his own Scotland Yard!"

To my surprise, Miss Gardiner turned white, and trembled as if beneath a blow. Even as I watched her, I saw also that Miss Lathrop was watching her, stealthily but closely.

Irene endeavored to speak further, but was unable to do so. Her quivering lips would utter no word, and as we looked at her in amazement, unable to guess what had so stirred her, Nurse Lathrop arose and taking Irene's arm, led her from the room.

"Whatever's the matter with Irene?" exclaimed Mr. Whiting. "Anybody would think she was shielding the man in the motor-car, instead of Milly! I tell you the whole thing hinges on that man, and I'm going to find him!"

"Will it,—will it be necessary to consult the police?" said Miss Maxwell, timidly, a little alarmed at Whiting's emphatic manner.

"Certainly not," said Mr. Maxwell. "Mr. Whiting's determination, and the skilled assistance of Mr. Hunt and Mr. King, can track that car quicker than all the police in the county. Go on, my boys, and may success go with you! But I will leave all questions of method and procedure to your judgment. I'm quite sure I could not help you; and if you'll excuse me, I would rather not take part in your planning."

I felt sure that this decision of Mr. Maxwell's was largely induced by his recognition of his sister's wishes. She was shrinkingly averse to having herself or her brother drawn into the actual investigation of the crime, and I think her gentle heart would have preferred that the criminal go unpunished, rather than take part in or even have cognizance of the sordid details of the search. And so I went with Tom Whiting and Mr. Hunt to the library to discuss what we should do first. The memory of what had happened there made it a ghastly place to converse in, but the fact that it was the scene of the crime, seemed to stir Whiting's mind to even a more intense determination to succeed in his quest.

"I propose," he said, "that we three canvass the neighborhood, and see if we can find anyone who saw that car Monday night."

"It may be a car belonging in the neighborhood," I suggested.

"Then we must find that out. At any rate this idea will do for a start."

We agreed to this, and after some further confab, in which Tom was the main spokesman, and Hunt took a very uninterested part, we set out on our preliminary search. Later on Whiting and I returned to Maxwell Chimneys, and found there a note from Hunt, saying that he had discovered nothing of consequence.

"Let's leave him out of it," said Whiting to me; "he's no sort of a detective, anyway, unless he's working on his own individual theory. What did you find out, King?"

As we mutually discovered, we had found out considerable. Sifted out and checked up, the evidence seemed to be, that the car described by the Earl was neither fiction nor imagination.

Mr. Plattner, the neighbor on the right,—though the country houses sat some distance apart,—had seen that car come from the village of Hamilton at about ten o'clock on Monday night. He had chanced to notice it because of its great speed, and he described it as a long gray car with several men in it.

Mr. Allen, the neighbor on the other side, had seen the car pass his house, going very fast, at some time after ten. His description was the same, and we couldn't doubt the identity of the car seen by the Earl and by these two neighbors. This made it pretty positive that a fast car had come up from the village at ten, had 'turned in and stopped at the Maxwells', and had gone on along the main road by or before half-past ten. The definiteness of this seemed to Whiting to be a long step toward our goal, and my half-formed doubts had no weight with him.

"But the man in the car couldn't have gone up on the veranda by that little outside staircase, without Miss Gardiner seeing him," I said.

"Don't you be too sure that Irene didn't see him," said Whiting; "that girl knows a whole lot more than Mildred about things, but there's no earthly use in trying to get anything out of her. Irene Gardiner is a sphinx and a sibyl and a siren and all such things, but as a witness she's absolutely worthless! She doesn't want to tell anything, and wouldn't tell it if she did! But she knows! O Lord, yes, that girl knows a lot!"

"Not guilty knowledge!" I cried.

"Depends on what you mean by guilty. She didn't shoot Philip, of course, but she knows a thing or two about who did."

I made no reply to this, for I was beginning to realize that I could not speak restrainedly when I tried to defend Irene.

So Whiting went on.

"Now let's go down to the village and see if that car didn't stop at the inn before coming up toward Mr. Plattner's. It would be a most natural thing to do."

So to the inn we went, taking for the purpose a little runabout from the Maxwell garage. The ample-faced inn-keeper listened to our questions and then said thoughtfully:

"Yep, I do seem to remember that there car. It stopped here along about half-past nine or a little later on Monday night. But I never once thought of connecting that up with the Maxwell murder! Land! do you think them men did it?"

"Did the men come in? How long did they stay?" said Whiting, impatiently.

"No, they didn't come in; they didn't hardly stop, as you might say. They jus' whizzed up here, stopped a minute, and asked me where the Maxwell place was."

"They did!" we cried, in amazed duet.

"Yes sir, they did! and of course I told 'em, and never thought of it again. Good land! so they wuz the murderers, was they?"

"We don't know," said Tom, "but we're going to find out, and we want you to help us all you can. Can you describe the car?"

"Well, of course, I'm mighty used to cars, as cars go,—but I couldn't just say the make of that one. It was long, extra-long, I should say,—and gray,—darkish gray. It was a touring car, and there were four young fellows in it beside the chauffeur. Now, that's jus' about all I know about it."

"Do you know the number?"

"Well, I didn't look at it purposely, but I most always glance at a number on general principles. But all I can tell you is, that the first two figures were sixes. The other three I couldn't swear to, though I'm 'most sure one of them was a four. Of course I only caught a glimpse of it, as they swung away, but I'd know that car again anywhere!"

"Well! we may want you to identify it, if we can find it anywhere. What were the men like?"

"I didn't notice them much. It was the chap that sat by the driver that asked me where the Maxwells lived. He was a big man, one of the biggest I ever saw, and with a big, deep voice and an off-hand way,—kind of like a Westerner. The whole crowd was off-hand; kind of laughin' and carryin' on, but I didn't pay much attention to 'em. If I'd a thought anything about it, I'd a thought they was some friends of the Maxwells, but I didn't even think that. If you hadn't brought it up, I'd never have thought of that car again! How are you going to find it?"

"That's just what I don't know," said Whiting, gloomily; "you see, King, we've lost so much time. The trails are all cold, the clues all destroyed, and I confess I don't know which way to look."

The inn-keeper looked on in sympathetic silence, his bland face devoid of any idea or suggestion. But I had an inspiration. "There's one thing, Whiting," I said; "if those men left the Maxwells' as late as half-past ten, they must have gone somewhere to spend the night. Of course, they would want to get pretty well away, but I doubt if they'd travel all night. Now, let's telephone to the most likely places, and see if they know anything about them."

"Now, that's a smart idea," commented Schwartz, the inn-keeper. "I can give you a list or a map of all the hotels and inns in this part of New Jersey."

"It's a pretty slim chance," said Whiting, but his face showed a gleam of hope.

"We've got to take slim chances," said I, "if we take any."

We called up a score of places on the telephone, and spent two good hours doing it. But at one of them we spotted our quarry. About midnight that gray motor-car had put up at a small hotel in Millville, a town some thirty miles away. The hotel man described the car and the party, and said that the man who registered was not the big Westerner, but one of the others, and who signed James Mordaunt and party.

We asked no further information over the wire, but determined to go to Millville early the next morning and learn what he could. Then, if we could trace our men, to go on wherever we might be led.

XVII: Big Jack Judson

WE went back to the house rather elated with our success; but when we told the others what we proposed to do, our plan did not meet with entire approval.

The Maxwells thought it a hopeless quest.

Edith Whiting said it could not possibly lead to anything worthwhile; and as for Hunt, he openly ridiculed the whole thing.

Miss Gardiner, too, endeavored to dissuade us.

"Why, Mr. King," she said, "it's utterly absurd to think you can find that car or those people after nearly a week has passed!"

"But we can at least try, Miss Gardiner," I said, wondering at her persistence.

"But what's the use, when you know you can't catch them?"

"What's the use of any endeavor? and there's always a chance that it may succeed."

"Well, then, may I go with you?"

"Why certainly," I replied; "so far as I'm concerned, I should be delighted to have you. Perhaps Mrs. Whiting will go, too."

We spent most of the evening in grave discussion. There was an undercurrent of disturbance that I could not understand. At one moment we would seem to be all working harmoniously in the same direction; and then one or another would fly off at a tangent with some inexplicable remark or criticism. But since Mr. Maxwell and his sister raised no real objection to our going—though they had little hope of its successful result,—I paid scant heed to others' advices.

Miss Gardiner's attitude bothered me most. She seemed determined to persuade us not to go, but she took no definite stand in the matter. She merely implied her opinions, and made vague suggestions that we might get into trouble by interfering with what was doubtless a party of young men on a pleasure trip.

"Even if that car did come in and go around the house and out again," said Miss Gardiner, almost angrily, "that doesn't prove the men criminals! Why, they might not even have known Philip or Mildred."

"But they asked the inn-keeper where the Maxwells lived," I reminded her.

"Probably because this is the show place of the town, and they wanted to see it," she retorted.

"But they wouldn't come at ten o'clock at night to see it," exclaimed Tom Whiting; "I don't know, Irene, why you're so afraid we'll find those men."

"I'm not afraid of any such thing," responded Miss Gardiner, with a rising color at the implied accusation.

"How should I know or care who the men are?"

"You were on the upper veranda when they came," went on Tom.

"And I have told you that I saw no one," and Irene spoke coldly; and rising, immediately left the room.

"Now she's mad," said Whiting, with a sigh; "but I do think that girl is holding something back."

"Oh, surely she can't know anything about it that she won't tell," said Miss Maxwell, looking anxious; "I can't bear to think Irene deceitful."

"She isn't deceitful," I declared; "I don't believe she knows anything she hasn't told, but if she does, you may depend upon it she is withholding it from right motives."

"I can't imagine any right motive for concealing the truth in a case like this," said Whiting, sternly.

"She may be shielding somebody else." Miss Lathrop said this in her most insinuating tones, and I at once had a conviction that she only said it to involve Irene. If so, I determined to call her bluff.

"Just what do you mean by that, Miss Lathrop?" I inquired; "if you know that Miss Gardiner is shielding somebody, surely you ought not to withhold the fact."

"I know nothing about Miss Gardiner," said the nurse, pursing her lips, primly; "it is not for me to have opinions on this matter at all."

"Quite so," I returned coolly, "I admit opinions are of little value; but if you know of any facts you should not conceal them."

"When I learn of any facts I will not conceal them," returned the nurse, and a gleam in her eye made me think that she looked forward hopefully to gaining such knowledge.

Next morning we started on our trip to Millville.

Miss Maxwell proposed that we take Miss Lathrop with us to give her some fresh air; and that she herself would sit with Milly in the absence of the nurse.

Miss Leslie was slowly regaining her strength, but was still prostrated from the effects of the shock, and also by the delayed healing of her wound. She was allowed to see no one except those who took care of her. Of course this necessitated the Whitings' continued stay at Maxwell Chimneys, and as

I was determined to see the case through, my stay was also indefinitely prolonged. As for Miss Gardiner, she declared each morning that she was going home that day, and each afternoon concluded to stay longer.

And so we started off for Millville; Tom Whiting and his wife in front, while I sat back with Miss Gardiner and the nurse.

It was a beautiful drive in the fresh morning air, and the roads were bordered with golden-rod and red sumac. The foliage was beginning to turn, and for a time the casual conversation was entirely regarding the weather and the scenery.

And then Miss Gardiner said abruptly, "Who is James Mordaunt?"

"I never heard of him before," I replied. "But you know he isn't the one who asked Schwartz where the Maxwells lived."

"What was his name?" demanded Irene in a nervous tone.

"I don't know I'm sure; that's what we hope to find out in Millville."

"I hope you won't," she exclaimed, and it seemed involuntary.

"Why?" I said, and Miss Lathrop said, "why?" at the same moment.

"Oh, I didn't exactly mean that, but I am so sure he can't be the criminal, that I hate to see you get on a wrong trail."

"I think that's rather a weak explanation of your speech, Miss Gardiner," said the nurse, with one of her most annoying smiles.

"Perhaps you can give a better explanation!" and Miss Gardiner's voice was coldly angry.

But I had no desire to listen to a feminine quarrel, and I said, pleasantly, "Miss Gardiner's speech doesn't need an explanation. Indeed, we're all so bewildered by our conflicting thoughts that I fear we sometimes talk at random."

"I fear some of us do," said Miss Lathrop, shortly.

But I diplomatically managed to keep peace between them, and at last we reached Millville. Our destination was the Prospect House, and we went directly there and interviewed the proprietor, Mr. Halkett, with whom we had talked over the telephone. He greeted us cordially, and took us at once to his private parlor. I told him frankly that we wanted to know the names of those men who were with Mr. Mordaunt, but I did not tell him why we were inquiring. He told us that only the one name was registered, but that during their stay he had learned the others. There were two men named Greene, and one, the big Western man, was Judson; and the chauffeur was Hopkins.

"That Judson's the man," I declared, "whose name we want. What's his first name?"

"John," said Mr. Halkett; "John Judson. But his comrades called him Jack or Juggins. They were a hearty lot of fellows, and all in gay spirits except big Judson."

"Wasn't he?" asked Whiting, eagerly.

"No," returned Mr. Halkett, "he was moody and silent; and when the other men tried to cheer him up, he would say, 'Let me alone, boys, I'm feeling down.'"

"How long were they here?" I inquired.

"Just over the one night. They arrived before midnight, last Monday night, and went away the next morning, about ten or eleven."

"Where did they go?"

"Well, I don't know exactly; but they seemed to be making a tour along the Southern New Jersey coast. I know they were going to Atlantic City and later to Cape May. They did say they'd stop here on their way back, but I never place much dependence on those promises. Young fellows often think they'll come back the same way and then they switch off to another road."

"Where were they from?" asked Whiting.

"Mordaunt registered from Philadelphia; and that big Judson was from out West. I don't know about the others."

We asked further questions, but none brought any more definite information. We didn't want to let Mr. Halkett know that we had any sinister reason for wanting to find these men, and he probably thought they had been speeding, or some such light offence as that. As we took our leave, I fell back a little, and whispered to Mr. Halkett that if the party should return, he was to telephone me at once and privately. This he agreed to do, and then we went back to Maxwell Chimneys.

Our conference at home after this trip was more amiable than the one the night before. Miss Gardiner seemed relieved that we had not traced the men; though I by no means felt inclined to drop our search for them, and I had my own notions of what I should do next.

Miss Lathrop made no unkind remarks, but I couldn't help observing that she watched Irene stealthily, and with much the same assured expression that a cat watches a mouse.

Mr. Maxwell merely observed that he couldn't believe Mr. Mordaunt was implicated in our tragedy, as he had never heard that name before. But when I went on to tell of big Jack Judson known by his friends as Juggins, both Mr. Maxwell and his sister exclaimed in surprise.

"That's the man!" declared Miss Maxwell; "Juggins is the man who shot our Philip! oh, how dreadful! and that's why he said, 'to think he should shoot me!' Mr. King, you have indeed found the criminal!" and Miss Miranda burst into such hysterical sobbing, that Miss Lathrop at once went over and took her in her arms.

"There, there, Miranda," said her brother, "don't jump at conclusions. It couldn't have been he! Why, there wasn't time for such a thing!"

Then he turned to us, and explained, "This Judson, or Juggins, as his classmates called him, was in Philip's class at college, but they never were friends. I don't know the reason, but there was a never healed feud between them. Philip stayed away from class re-union because he didn't wish to meet Judson. I never forced my boy's confidence, and he never told me what it was all about, but I know they were enemies. My sister knows it, too, and that is why she now suspects this man of the crime. But I cannot think it. I can't believe that Judson came here secretly, and shot my boy down in cold blood! No, Mr. King, I cannot think we have the criminal yet."

This speech amazed me. If Judson were Phil's enemy, if he came to Hamilton that night and asked where the Maxwells lived, if his car, or the car he was in, was seen to enter and leave Maxwell Chimneys at the time of the murder,—what more evidence, save the man's own confession, could be required? And the hotel man in Millville had told us that Judson was sad and gloomy, though his companions were merry.

Surely then, the others didn't know it, but Judson had stopped at Maxwell Chimneys just long enough to commit his dreadful deed and had then gone on with them. I repeated all this to Mr. Maxwell, but he only shook his head. "Not likely," he said, "not likely. It was too sudden, too quickly done, to be even a possibility. And, too, though they were not friends, there could not have been such bitter hatred as to culminate in murder. And they hadn't met for years."

"You don't know that, Mr. Maxwell," I argued; "they may have met elsewhere than here, or they may have corresponded. At any rate the circumstances are too suspicious to be ignored. Judson must be found and questioned, if only to give him the chance of clearing himself."

"I suppose that is so," agreed Mr. Maxwell; beginning to take a more rational view of the case; "Go ahead then, Mr. King, in your own way. I will not interfere. But don't accuse Judson without giving him a chance to explain himself."

I promised this, and then I went away to confer with Hunt as to this new development.

It was about seven o'clock that same evening, when, as I chanced to be alone in the music-room, Miss Lathrop came to me, and as she approached put her finger to her lip in a warning manner.

"I must speak to you alone, Mr. King," she whispered. "We are alone," I answered, a little coldly, for her manner irritated me.

"Yes," she said, "if we're not interrupted. Now listen, while I tell you something."

"I am listening," I said, really annoyed by her important and mysterious manner."

"Don't be so rude! you'll change your tune when you hear what I have to tell you."

"What have you to tell me?" I asked, more gently, for I suddenly realized that if I antagonized her, I might miss some real information.

"Only this. Miss Gardiner has just mailed a letter addressed to Mr. John Judson."

"What?"

"Don't speak so loud! It is just as I tell you. So you see they are colleagues!"

"They are what?"

"Do stop asking absurd questions,—you heard me! I tell you because I think you ought to know, that Miss Gardiner is in correspondence with that man."

"She isn't in correspondence with him!"

"Well, she has just written him, at any rate; and she must be in correspondence with him or how could she know his address?"

"What is his address?"

"The letter is directed to him at Cape May."

I had recovered from my first dazed bewilderment, and though still angry, I knew it was better not to show this. Moreover, if what the nurse told me was true, as of course it must be, I must find out all I could from her.

"How do you know this? You've been prying into Miss Gardiner's private affairs!"

"Is not that allowable if one is tracking a murderer?"

I could not restrain my anger entirely. "I didn't know you were officially employed in this matter," I flung at her.

"Nor am I," she said, proudly; "if my voluntary assistance is scorned, I will discontinue it."

She turned away, and I saw I was defeating my own ends.

"Wait a moment, Miss Lathrop," I begged; "I ask your pardon if I have offended you, but I'm nearly at my wits' end in this matter, and your revelation is indeed a surprise to me. How did you discover this letter?"

"I happened to take a letter myself to the mail box in the hall, and I found the footman just emptying the box to take the letters to the post office. I chanced to see the name Judson on one of them, and naturally it caught my eye. So I looked at the letter, and saw that it was in Miss Gardiner's handwriting. I noted the address, and I said nothing to anyone else, but brought the information directly to you. Have I done right?"

"You have certainly done right in telling me about it, Miss Lathrop. May I ask you not to mention it to anyone else,—at least not for the present?"

"I will not mention it," said Miss Lathrop, and then she glided swiftly away, and I was left to ponder on her astonishing news. But after only a short consideration, I decided to go at once to Miss Gardiner and ask for the truth. There could be no ordinary or innocent reason why she should be corresponding with the man we suspected of crime.

She must have concealed knowledge of some sort, whether guilty or not. It was nearly dinner time, but I sent a message to her asking her to see me at once for a moment in the music-room.

She came down almost immediately, and as she entered, though her manner was cold and distant, I thought I had never seen her look more beautiful. Her soft, trailing, black gown was most becoming, and a gauzy black scarf that veiled her white shoulders seemed to add to her dignity and hauteur.

"You sent for me?" she said, without a smile, and in low, level tones.

"I did," I replied, "and I'm going to tell you frankly, why I did so. I have learned, Miss Gardiner, that you have just sent a letter to Mr. John Judson."

"Have I not a right to send letters to whom I choose?"

"You certainly have. But when such a letter proves that you know the address of the man we are looking for, I have a right to ask you what you know of him, and why you conceal from us the fact that you do know him."

"And if you have a right to ask those questions, I also have a right to refuse to answer them."

"You have that right, but is it wise to exercise it, Miss Gardiner? Please drop this antagonistic attitude, and if you're not willing to help us in our search, won't you tell me why?"

"I'm not willing to help you in your search, and I refuse to tell you why."

Miss Gardiner spoke deliberately, and turning slowly, left the room. It may have been my imagination, but I thought she hesitated an instant at the doorway, as if half hoping I would call her back. But I did not do so, as I knew it was but a few moments before dinner time, and I quickly concluded to wait until the evening, and then endeavor to get her alone for a more protracted interview.

All through the meal I was pre-occupied and found it difficult to control my thoughts sufficiently to take part in the general conversation. Moreover, when I lifted my eyes, I invariably found either Miss Gardiner or Miss Lathrop regarding me intently, and I found it embarrassing to meet their gaze.

XVIII: A Pistol Shot

DINNER was nearly over when I was called to the telephone. Excusing myself from the table, I answered the summons, only to find that it was Mr. Halkett, of the Millville Hotel, who wished to speak to me.

His message was of importance, for it told me that the gray car and the four men of Mordaunt's party had returned to the Prospect House, on their way back to Philadelphia.

"Why, I thought they had gone to Cape May," I said, impulsively.

"They did intend to," replied Mr. Halkett, "but they changed their plan, and they're here for the night. They're going to stay here until eleven o'clock or so to-morrow morning. They don't know I'm telling you this, as that's according to your orders."

"All right, Mr. Halkett," I said, seriously; "don't let them know you've telephoned me; for, understand, this is an important matter. On no account raise their suspicions in any way, but see to it that they don't leave any earlier than eleven tomorrow morning."

"All right, Mr. King; I'll see to that."

I went back to the table, intending to tell them all what I had just heard, but on second thoughts I decided not to. So I said nothing about it until after dinner, when I told Tom Whiting only.

I also told him about Irene's letter to Judson, proving that she had thought him at Cape May, whereas the party were on their return trip. He agreed with me that the situation had grown serious, and that we must move carefully.

We concluded to say nothing to anyone, but to go alone next morning over to Millville. Of course, I gave up my idea of another interview with Irene that night, as I wanted to keep her unaware of the fact that Judson was at Millville. Nor did I tell Hunt, as it seemed to me that Whiting and I could handle the case best alone. So next morning, immediately after breakfast, we started. The little runabout was a swift car, and we had ample time to reach Millville by ten o'clock. But just at the last moment, indeed, as I was getting into the car, Miss Lathrop ran out to speak to me.

"I couldn't get a chance to tell you before," she whispered; "but Miss Gardiner has sent that Judson man another letter! She had it mailed late last night, and it was addressed to Millville, and it had a special delivery stamp on it."

"Thank you, Miss Lathrop," I said, and for once I was honestly grateful to her.

"Speed her up, Tom!" I said, as I swung into the little car beside Whiting; "we've a new reason for haste. Get over to Millville as quick as you can. Irene has sent that man another letter, and he'll get away from us yet!"

"Great Scott, King!" said Tom, as we took a higher speed; "what is that girl up to? You know, King, there's nothing crooked about Irene."

"Then she's coerced or threatened by that villain Judson," I declared. "He's the murderer, Tom, and Irene knows it!"

"Oh, no, no! not so bad as that! Well, anyhow, we'll soon find out."

We said little more as we tore along the miles. My thoughts were busy with this sudden new surprise. How had Irene discovered that Judson was in Millville, when a few hours before she had thought him at Cape May? To be sure she might have had a letter or telegram in the meantime; or,—and what was more likely the case,—she had heard enough of my telephoning to realize that the Mordaunt party were back at Millville and to act accordingly.

On we flew, and I said no word to Tom, lest I distract his attention from his driving. Moreover, I knew the situation must mystify him quite as much as it did me.

After an incredibly short trip, we whirled in at the hotel entrance. Only to be met by a distracted proprietor, who told us the car had just left with the Mordaunt party.

"But I told you not to let them get away!" I thundered, in mad disappointment.

"I know it, Mr. King," said Halkett, apologetically, "but I couldn't help it. I had to go over to the bank on an important matter and when I came back the party had just gone. Of course I couldn't forcibly restrain them."

"No, I suppose you couldn't. Which way did they go?"

"That way. The main road to Philadelphia."

"Turn around, Tom! chase them! it's our only chance."

Whiting swung the car around, and we flew out of the gate and along the main road.

"There's little hope," I shouted at him, as we whizzed madly on, "but if they've had tire trouble or anything, we might overtake them. Anyway, we'll have a try at it for a few miles,—and then give it up, if we have to."

Whiting fully entered into the spirit of the thing, and we went faster than I had ever before traveled in a motor-car.

The little machine rocked, and I involuntarily grasped at the side of the seat, lest I be flung out. Fortunately the road was clear, and of course a good one, and we kept on. I was just about ready to cry quits, when we saw a car ahead of us.

And, moreover, it was the car!

"That's it, Tom!" I shouted; "speed her!"

He couldn't speed her any more than he was already doing, but as we had gained on the big car, I believed we could continue to gain.

And we did! Of course Mordaunt's car was not going at top speed, as they didn't know they were being pursued,—a fact which I hoped they would not discover.

But they did discover it. Whether a case of a guilty conscience or not, a man rose from his seat in the tonneau, and turned to look backward.

He saw us, and must have realized that we were chasing them, for they immediately began to go faster.

The big car sped ahead, and we followed.

"Speed her, Tom!" I cried; "whoop her up!"

"Can't do any more," Tom replied; "this is our best." The poor fellow was straining every nerve, and bent to his wheel in a frenzy of excitement.

The man in the car ahead was still standing, and looking backward at us.

The space between the cars lengthened slowly, and I realized that soon they would spin ahead out of our sight. I said nothing to Tom, for I knew he could not get another ounce of speed out of our car.

The big man who stood gazing at us, as the touring car streaked ahead, was doubtless Jack Judson. He was an enormous man, and swung his arms with the free movement of a Westerner.

Though I could not see his features distinctly, I felt the triumphant smile on his face, as he took off his soft, flapping hat and waved it at us in farewell.

But even as be replaced that hat, I saw his face more clearly, and I suddenly realized that this meant a lessening of the distance between us!

"Tom!" I fairly yelled in his ear; "they're slowing down! they don't mean to,—but something has happened! we're gaining on them! Never mind, boy, don't even look up,—just saw wood!"

Obediently Tom watched his wheel, and I stared at the car, to which we were certainly creeping nearer. Yes, slowly but steadily nearer, and now I could discern Judson's face clearly, and could see his baffled expression give way to one of new resolve.

Stooping an instant, the big man straightened up again, and now in his right hand he held what was unmistakably a deadly sharp shooter!

"Tom!" I cried, actually more alarmed for my unconscious companion than for myself; "Tom,—duck! he's going to shoot us!"

In my excitement, I didn't think of ducking myself, and I sat spellbound, gazing at that weapon aimed surely at us, while Tom, after one glance, dropped his head in an effort to shield himself.

The next instant a report rang out, and as the big car passed out of sight, our pace slackened and we went along limpingly.

The big Westerner had cleverly and purposely punctured one of our front tires!

After the report, Tom's head came up, and he evidently expected, as he was unhurt, to see me wounded or dead beside him.

His look of amazement was almost comical, when I said, "He shot at the tire, Whiting, not at us, and with his blooming Western skill, he hit it!"

He had done just that, and now there was nothing for us to do, but to get out and mend the tire and then go home.

We did so, and though we talked the matter over all the way home, we could come to no other conclusion than that Judson was the murderer and that he had escaped us.

"I shall put it straight up to Miss Gardiner," I declared; "she knows about this thing and she must be made to tell."

"She must know about it," said Whiting, "but I can't believe yet that she is willfully shielding a murderer. It must be from some mistaken sense of duty or loyalty to someone."

"She's certainly very much interested in this man Judson," I returned, a little gloomily. I was really under the spell of Miss Gardiner's fascination, and of course I hoped she could clear up all these uncertainties, but certainly the Judson affair looked ominous.

After luncheon that day, I made a special request of Miss Gardiner that she would confer with Tom Whiting and myself. She agreed willingly enough, and we went to the music-room for our talk. We had thought it better not to tell the rest of the household about our morning's experience until after the conference with Irene. So I had told Mr. Maxwell that the Mordaunt party had left the hotel before we reached there and told him nothing more. But he discerned somehow, that there was more to the story, and he joined us in the music-room, uninvited. As there was no real reason why he shouldn't know all about it, I was quite willing he should be there.

In consideration of his deafness, we all sat near together and spoke distinctly.

"To begin with," I said, "I'm positive that John Judson is the man who shot Philip and Mildred."

"And I am equally positive he did not!" declared Irene, her eyes blazing; "and I can prove it!"

"You can!" exclaimed Tom Whiting; "what do you know, Irene, that the rest of us don't know? and why are you willing to defeat the efforts of right and justice?"

"First tell me what happened this morning," said the girl.

So I gave a rapid account of our pursuit of the Mordaunt car, and of Judson's shooting our tire in order to make his own escape.

"Then he got away safely?" asked Irene, eagerly.

"Yes, he is now well on toward Philadelphia. Are you glad he escaped?"

"I certainly am, as the man is absolutely innocent of any connection with our mystery."

"You know this Judson, then, Miss Gardiner?" asked Mr. Maxwell.

"Yes, I know him very well."

"Then you know he was an enemy to Philip?"

"Not exactly an enemy, though I know they never liked each other. But since Mr. Judson is safely away, I will tell you the whole story. He has been a friend of mine for some years, and though he has asked me several times to marry him, I have always refused him. Last week he went to see me at my home in New York, and they told him I was down here. He was making a motor trip with Mr. Mordaunt, and on their way to Atlantic City, they stopped here at Mr. Judson's request. He wrote me that he wanted to see me once more before he went West, but he did not care to meet Philip. So I wrote him that I would be on the upper veranda Monday night at ten o'clock, and that he might come up by the little outside staircase, and thus he need not see Philip at all. He did this, and it was Mr. Mordaunt's car that the Earl saw that night."

"Then Judson did come up on the upper veranda, Monday night at ten o'clock," said Tom Whiting; "and yet you say he had nothing to do with the shooting!"

"Absolutely nothing," said Irene. "We were on the other side of the house from the library, and he remained with me not more than two minutes."

"Why such a short stay?" asked Tom.

"Because,—because I was crying when he came, and I didn't want to see him anyway, and I begged him to go away at once."

"At what time was this?"

"I don't know exactly, but it was quite some time after ten. In fact, Mr. King came and told me about Philip and Mildred, very soon after Mr. Judson went away. But I can swear, if necessary, that he only came up to see me, stayed but a few moments and went away again. He did not go round to the library side of the house at all."

"What were you crying about?" asked Whiting, gently. "I was upset and nervous, and I couldn't control myself."

"You have heard from Mr. Judson since?" asked Mr. Maxwell, who was paying close attention to Irene's story.

"Yes,—and of course he has heard of the murder, but he has no idea he was suspected of it. But I wanted him to get away, for to detain him and make inquiries, would only mean trouble for an innocent man. So I wrote him at Millville that you were going over there, and begged him to get away before you came. I think he must have been mystified at my urging him to a speedy departure, but I'm glad to know that he did as I advised him."

"It is a strange story, Miss Gardiner," said Mr. Maxwell, thoughtfully, "but of course I do not doubt your word."

"You need not," said Irene, haughtily. "I have told only the exact truth. If I have concealed this episode, it is only because I didn't wish Mr. Judson's name brought into question at all."

We talked for some time after this, and we all agreed that as Judson was now entirely out of it, we must look in some other direction.

"I don't think Mr. Hunt is doing much," said Whiting, "and I think, Mr. Maxwell, it would be wise to put the whole affair in the hands of the police."

"If you think best," said the old gentleman, hopelessly. "I think myself, that Mr. Hunt is not discovering anything, but that may not be his fault. As I told you, Tom, whatever you and Peter agree upon, I will agree to. But I cannot seem to take any initiative. I am too old, and my deafness stands in my way, when I would question anybody."

"Certainly, Mr. Maxwell," said I, "you could not be expected to take up this matter personally. I'll see Hunt again, and if he agrees, I think we will give it over to the police."

But before I saw Hunt, I determined to do a little more investigating by myself. I went up to the library, hoping that from the scene of the crime I could get some hint of which direction to turn.

Of course, too much time had elapsed to look for further clues, but as I sat there, something brought back to my mind the black spangles I had found that next morning. The maid who had found the Earl's seal must have overlooked the tiny spangles as I found them later. But she might have found others of the same sort when she dusted the room, and I determined to ask her.

I went in search of her, and showing her the spangles I had, I inquired if she had seen any like them in the library the morning she had found the seal. At first she couldn't remember, and then she recollected having picked up two or three near the window.

"Have you any idea," I said, "where they could have come from? Did any of the ladies wear a spangled dress that night?"

"Oh, I know where they have come from," she said, quickly; "they are from the fan of Miss Gardiner."

"How do you know?"

"Because Miss Gardiner carried the black fan that evening. She left it on a seat on the veranda, and I found it and put it again in her room."

"You are certain, Emily, that Miss Gardiner carried the fan that evening?"

"I am sure, Mr. King."

"That is all, Emily, you may go."

Here was something definite. For I remembered distinctly that Miss Gardiner went to her room to get that fan just before she and I walked together on the upper veranda. Then I left her, and she remained up there, and Judson found her there, crying.

Meantime, some spangles from that fan had been dropped by the library window! It seemed to me positive proof that Irene had been around there between half past nine and half past ten that night. The more I thought it over the more I was convinced that it must be so. And yet, I did not like to face her with these facts and ask an explanation. But it seemed to me that I must do this, before going any further.

So I went on my very distasteful errand, and found Miss Gardiner in the music-room with Miss Maxwell.

"You know," I said, speaking to the girl, "it is our duty to investigate every possible clue."

"Of course," said Irene, but she trembled nervously and seemed to apprehend some new disclosure.

"Then I will show you these spangles," I said, taking them from my pocketbook, "and ask you if they could have dropped from a fan of yours."

Irene looked at them, and said, quietly, "I have a black spangled fan; they may very likely have dropped from it."

"Did you carry it the Monday night that Philip died?"

"I may have done so; I don't remember exactly. Why?"

"Because these spangles were found in the library, the morning after the shooting."

"And you think that turns suspicion toward me?" Irene rose, and stood with flashing eyes, the embodiment of indignation and anger.

"You are entirely mistaken, Mr. King, as to your suspicions! They may be spangles from my fan, they may have been dropped in the library; but I was in and out of that room during the early evening, long before the time of the tragedy."

"But you didn't have the fan with you, then," I persisted; "because I remember you went to your room for it, when you and I were together after our dance."

Miss Gardiner turned perfectly white, and swayed as if about to faint. Miss Maxwell sprang to her aid, and putting an arm about her led her from the room.

"I can't have this poor girl tortured, Peter," said the gentle old lady, and they went away leaving me to face a new suspicion that was as unwelcome as it was unexpected.

XIX: Red Ink Spots

I RESOLVED to say nothing more about the fan or the spangles to any member of the household, but to lay the case before Hunt, when he came over to the house the next morning.

To my surprise he did not seem at all impressed with the idea of Miss Gardiner being implicated.

"You let your idea of clues run away with you, Mr. King," he said. "To be sure the spangles may point in Miss Gardiner's direction, but she certainly cannot be the intruder who came in the motor coat and cap. Now, it seems to me if we're going to look for our man through any clues, we'd better consider that red ink. When Miss Leslie threw that inkstand, and so much ink was spilled on the rug, it is extremely probable that some also spattered on the coat of the assailant."

"Well, it seems to me," I said, "that that's about the most elusive clue you could think of! We can't possibly, after all these days, trace a motor coat with red ink spots on it."

"He might have taken it to a cleaner's," said Hunt, thoughtfully.

"Then shall we advertise for a cleaner who has had such a job recently?"

But my sarcasm was lost upon Hunt. "I doubt if a cleaner could take out such spots," he went on; "red ink is almost indelible."

"Well, I have little hope of finding these mythical spots on a mythical coat belonging to a mythical man!"

"You're wrong there, for certainly the coat and the man are not mythical. Miss Leslie saw them. Perhaps she can tell us if the red ink spattered him," said Hunt, hopefully.

"She can't tell us anything at present. The doctor won't let her be spoken to on this subject. It seems to me, Hunt, the only thing to do is to call in the police. Of course if they find the man and the coat, some red ink spots on it would go a long way toward proving his guilt. But I'm sure that to find the man will require the skill of the police force, rather than our ineffectual attempts."

"Perhaps you're right," agreed Hunt, "but all the same I shall try to find that coat." Then Tom Whiting and his wife appeared at the library door.

"We want you, Mr. King, if Mr. Hunt will excuse you," said Edith Whiting, in her pleasant way.

"Certainly," said Mr. Hunt. "I am just going home anyway."

"Have you discovered anything new?" asked Tom Whiting.

"We hope to do so," said Mr. Hunt.

"I think we are on the right track, though we have not progressed very far, as yet."

"We want you to go with us for a motor ride, Mr. King," said Edith Whiting to me.

"Tom insists on my going, and we are taking Irene with us."

We started away, but Hunt called me back to whisper a parting message.

"If you find any strangers in automobile togs," he said, "observe carefully whether there are any signs of their having tried to erase red ink spots from the lower fronts of their coats."

"That's the slimmest kind of a slim chance yet," I said, almost smiling at the idea, "but I promise you if I find an automobilist spattered with red ink, I will arrest him at once."

I found the others ready and waiting for me. It seemed pathetic to ride away in Philip's big automobile, but, as Tom Whiting had said, the ladies really needed some fresh air, and he thought the trip would do us all good.

Mr. Maxwell and Miss Miranda insisted on our going, and so we started off. Mr. and Mrs. Whiting sat in front, for Tom was quite as good a chauffeur as Philip had been; and Miss Gardiner and I sat behind. As there was ample room for another, Irene proposed that we stop for Gilbert Crane. This we did, and he seemed glad to accept the invitation.

It scarcely seemed like the same party who a few days before, accompanied by Philip, had traveled so merrily over these same roads.

On our return, Mrs. Whiting asked Mr. Crane to come in to luncheon with us, and he accepted. He alighted before I did, and as he stood waiting to help Miss Gardiner out, the midday sunlight shone full upon him.

I looked at him curiously, thinking what a large, fine-looking fellow he was physically, and how becoming his fashionable automobile coat was to him. Its color was a light brownish gray, and as my eye rested idly upon it, I suddenly noticed something that made my heart stand still.

On the front of this same coat, on the lower edge, were several small spots, visible only in the brightest sunlight, which, whatever they might be, had every appearance of being red ink.

To say I was stunned would pretty well express my feelings, but I was learning not to show surprise at unexpected developments.

I went into the house with the rest, and finding that Mr. Hunt had gone, I sent a note to him, by one of the servants, asking him to return at two o'clock.

He came just as we finished luncheon, and bidding him go in the library and await me there, I went into Mr. Maxwell's study. Finding my host there as I had hoped, and not wishing to elevate my voice, I scribbled on a bit of paper a request that Mr. Maxwell would ask Mr. Crane to come into his study, and would keep him there, securely, for twenty minutes at least.

Mr. Maxwell read the paper quietly, handed it back to me, gave me a quick nod of comprehension, and immediately went in search of Gilbert Crane. A moment later, I saw him return with Gilbert Crane. They entered the study and closed the door, so I knew that the coast was clear, and that for twenty minutes I need fear no interruption from them.

Eagerly seizing his coat from the hat-stand where he had flung it, I hastened to the library. I found Hunt there, and after closing the door I held up the coat for his inspection.

"You don't mean to say you have found the man!" he cried.

"I don't know about that," I said, very soberly, "but I have certainly found a coat that ought to be looked after. What do you make of this?"

I held the front of the coat toward the window to catch the bright sunlight, and drew Hunt's attention to the almost invisible spots on it. He looked at them in silence a moment, and then said abruptly: "Get some more blotters."

We dampened the blotters and applied them very carefully, for the spots were faint, and the surface of the cloth dusty. But the results showed strong evidence that the stains were similar to those on the carpet.

"Whose coat is it?" said Hunt, though I think he knew.

"Gilbert Crane's," I answered, looking straight at the detective.

"But that does not prove that Gilbert Crane committed the murder," he responded, looking at me with equal directness.

"It does not," I said, emphatically, "but it is certainly a clue that must lead somewhere."

"And we must follow it wherever it leads."

"Yes," I assented, "now that we have something to work on, let us get to work. Shall I call Crane up here, and ask him if he can explain these spots on his coat? Somehow, I can't help thinking that he could do so."

"Not yet," said Mr. Hunt. "I think it wiser to straighten out a few points before we speak to Mr. Crane on the subject. He is a peculiar man, and I don't want to antagonize him. I would much rather, if you please, that you would replace the coat where you found it, let Mr. Maxwell know that he need not detain Mr. Crane any longer, and then bring Miss Gardiner back here with you for a short consultation."

I followed Mr. Hunt's suggestions to the letter, but it was with a rapidly sinking heart. Not for a moment did I think Gilbert Crane a villain, and yet there were many circumstances that looked dark against him. I was also disturbed at Mr. Hunt's request for Irene. A strange foreboding made me fear that some dreadful revelation was about to take place.

The jury had rendered its verdict of "willful murder by a person unknown," and I fervently hoped the criminal might remain forever unknown rather than that the shadow of guilt might fall on anyone who had been hospitably received at Maxwell Chimneys.

Still, in the cause of justice, every possibility must be considered, and I knew that Mr. Hunt would shirk no duty, but would doggedly follow any clue that presented itself. I looked in at the study door, and the merest lifting of my eye-brows was sufficient to inform Mr. Maxwell that a detention of Gilbert was no longer necessary. I looked at young Crane's inscrutable face, and was obliged to admit to myself that it was not a frank countenance in its general effect. But I resolved that this fact should not be allowed to prejudice me against him. Finding Mrs. Whiting in the hall, and learning from her that Miss Gardiner had gone to her own room, I asked her to say to Miss Gardiner that Mr. Hunt desired to see her in the library. Mrs. Whiting promised to send Irene there at once, and, greatly dreading the interview, I returned to the library myself.

I found Hunt making a tabulated statement of certain facts.

"You see, Mr. King," he said, with a very grave face, "while these things are not positively incriminating, they are serious questions which need clearing up.

"Granting that the bronze horse was thrown at the intruder and replaced on the desk before you entered the room that night, we must allow that it was picked up and replaced by somebody. Miss Leslie was incapable of this act, the murderer was not likely to do it.

"Gilbert Crane was the first to find out that the tragedy had occurred. There is no witness to say what he might or might not have done in this room. It is possible therefore that he restored the horse to its place."

"And the inkstand?"

"You remember that Gilbert Crane insisted on spending the night in this house. Is it not, therefore, conceivable that he should have waited until everyone else had gone home, or retired to their rooms, and that he should then have come to the library, found the empty stand, refilled it, and replaced it?"

"But," said I, in utter amazement, "if he did not commit the crime why should he be so careful about these details?"

"I am not sure," said Mr. Hunt in a low voice, "that he did not commit the crime."

XX: Irene Tells the Truth

ALTHOUGH horrified and even indignant at Mr. Hunt's assertion, I could not fail to be impressed by his arguments. I was still bewildered at the possibilities he suggested, when a tap was heard at the library door. Mr. Hunt rose quietly and admitted Miss Gardiner.

The girl looked haggard and worn. Her brilliant coloring seemed faded, and her whole attitude betrayed deep distress not unmixed with fear.

But all of this she tried to hide beneath a mask of impassivity.

I think she impressed Hunt with her appearance of calmness, though I felt sure that her turbulent spirit was far from placid.

"Sit down, Miss Gardiner," said Hunt kindly. "I wish to ask you a few questions."

Irene sat down, and with an air both haughty and dignified awaited the detective's next words. Had it not been for her restless, troubled eyes, she would have deceived me into thinking her assumed indifference real.

"In your testimony, Miss Gardiner," began Mr. Hunt, "you declared that you did not leave the spot where you were sitting, on the east end of the balcony, the night of the murder, until you came into the house at about half past ten. Are you still prepared to swear to this statement?"

"Why should I not be, Mr. Hunt?" said Irene, but her lips grew white, and her voice trembled.

"You might have since recollected that you did go around to the west side, if only for a moment."

"I have no recollections that cause me to change my sworn statement in any way," declared Irene. Her voice had sunk almost to a whisper and her eyes refused to meet mine.

Mr. Hunt continued: "Were you around on the west side, near the library window, at any time during the evening— earlier, perhaps, than the time you spent sitting alone on the east side?"

"No," said Irene, and this time her voice was stronger and her whole air more decided, as she looked the detective straight in the eye. "I was not on the west balcony earlier in the evening. I was not there at all!"

The last sentence came with a desperate burst of emphasis, that somehow did not carry conviction. For some reason the girl was under a severe tension, and I couldn't help thinking there was danger of her physical collapse.

"Then," said Mr. Hunt, suddenly producing the black spangles—"then may I ask, Miss Gardiner, how these chanced to be found in the library, and on the library window-shutter?"

Irene Gardiner gave a low cry, and hiding her face in her hands, seemed in immediate danger of the collapse I had feared.

"Miss Gardiner," I said, for though her actions were inexplicable, I was still deeply under the spell of her fascination, and greatly desired to help her— "Miss Gardiner, let me advise you, as a friend, to tell your story frankly and truthfully. I am sure it will be better for all concerned."

Raising her head, Irene Gardiner flashed a look at me so full of faith and gratitude, that, assured of her complete innocence, I determined to become her strong ally.

"Oh!" she exclaimed, "I would be so glad to tell the truth! I swore to a falsehood from a sense of duty to another."

"It is always a mistaken sense of duty that leads to false swearing," said Mr. Hunt.

"I believe that is so," said Irene earnestly, "but I had no one to advise me and I thought I was doing right. The truth is, then, that I did go around to the west end of the balcony, and that I did look in at the library window."

"At what time was this?" asked Mr. Hunt.

"I don't know," said Irene, "but it was just before Mr. Judson came, and about ten minutes later Mr. King came to me on the front balcony, and told me what had happened."

"What did you see in the library?" asked Mr. Hunt.

"Must I tell that?"

"You must."

"Then I saw Philip lying on the floor, and Mildred fallen to the floor also. But she was partly hidden by the desk."

"Is that all you saw?" asked Mr. Hunt, looking at her intently. "Was there no one else in the room?"

"Must I tell that?" asked Irene again, with an appealing glance at me.

"Yes," said Mr. Hunt sternly, "much may depend on your telling the absolute truth."

"Then," said Irene, "I saw Mr. Crane placing a pistol in Mildred's hand."

"Wait," said I, "was this occurring just as you arrived at the window?"

"Yes."

"Then," I went on, "you cannot swear that he was placing the pistol in her hand. He might have been taking it away from her, or attempting to do so."

"I never thought of that," said Irene, an expression of relief lighting up her face.

"Even so," said Mr. Hunt, "he should have told of the incident in his own testimony. What did you do next, Miss Gardiner?"

"I went away at once. I went to the east side of the veranda. I was so mystified and horrified by what I had just seen that I flung myself into a chair and cried. I was still crying when, soon after, Mr. Judson came in search of me. And I was still crying when Mr. King came later to tell me what had happened."

"She was," I said, "and crying so violently that I was alarmed. But as Miss Maxwell appeared almost immediately, I left the two ladies to look after each other."

"And had it not been for the incriminating spangles, did you not intend to correct your misstatement?" said Mr. Hunt, looking at her severely.

"No," said Irene, and her manner now was frank and self-assured, "for I felt sure Mr. Crane had done nothing wrong, and I did not wish to attract any unfounded suspicions toward him."

"A suspicion that is really unfounded can do no one any harm," said Mr. Hunt, who seemed to be in a mood for oracular utterances.

"I am glad," said Irene simply, "for I would not wish any harm to come to Mr. Crane through my testimony."

"That is as it may be," said Mr. Hunt, and the interview was at an end. Although Irene's evidence had placed Gilbert in a doubtful position, I was not yet willing to believe the man guilty, or even that he was implicated in the crime.

Indeed, I was for going straight to him, and asking him for the explanation which I felt sure he could give. But Mr. Hunt did not agree with me. He was in the grasp of a new theory, and therefore subject to the temptation which too often assails a detective, to make the facts coincide with it.

"No," he said, "don't let us go ahead too rapidly. Let us formulate a definite proposition, and then see if we are warranted in assuming it to be a true one. In the first place, whoever killed Philip Maxwell must have had a strong personal motive for the deed.

"There is no reason to suspect an ordinary burglar, for there is nothing whatever to indicate burglary in the whole affair. If Philip Maxwell had any personal enemies, the fact is not known to us. Even his uncle is unaware of the existence of any such."

"The only man we know of who might have had an ill-feeling toward Philip Maxwell—mind, I say, might have had—is Gilbert Crane. We know that an antagonism existed between the two men on account of Miss Leslie. While it would not seem to us that this antagonism was sufficient to develop a crime, yet parallel cases are not unknown. Gilbert Crane is a man of deep passions, fiery temper, and uncontrollable impulses.

"He is erratic, eccentric, and, while I do not wish to judge him too harshly, I must admit he seems to be of the stuff of which villains are made."

"But none of this is definitely incriminating," I said, appalled at the sudden directness of Hunt's attack.

"No," he replied, "and that is why I'm not willing to proceed as if. it were, or as if I so considered it."

"It is absurd anyway," I said almost angrily, "for you know that he was in the billiard-room at exactly ten o'clock. I saw him there myself. And according to Miss Maxwell, the shots were fired at ten o'clock."

"Yes, according to Miss Maxwell. But it has occurred to me that hers is the only evidence that the shots were fired at ten o'clock, and we are by no means certain that her clock or watch was exactly right."

"The clock in the study was right," I said doggedly, "it always is. Mr. Maxwell is very particular about that."

"Yes, but ladies are not apt to be so exact with their timepieces. At any rate, I shall make it my business to find out."

"Let us find out now," I said eagerly.

"If there is anything in this horrible theory I want to know it at once."

"Go yourself," said Hunt. "Go at once, and ask Miss Maxwell as to the accuracy of her clock."

I found Miss Maxwell alone, and I asked her in a casual manner how she knew it was ten o'clock when she heard, or thought she heard, the two pistol shots.

"It was ten by the little clock on my dressing table," she replied.

"I am sure of that, for it was striking at the time I heard the reports."

"And is that clock always right?" I asked.

"No," she said; "in fact, it is almost never right. For some time I have been intending to have it regulated."

"Is it slow or fast?" I asked, trying to preserve my casual manner.

"It runs slow," she said, "and that night it must have been as much as ten minutes slow, because I remember I was late for dinner, though I thought I was in ample time."

"You should have stated this discrepancy sooner, Miss Maxwell," I said, unable to keep a note of grave concern out of my voice.

"Why," she returned, in astonishment.

"I had no idea that would make any difference. In fact, I didn't think anything about it. How can it make any difference?"

"Never mind, Miss Maxwell," I said soothingly, "perhaps it won't make any difference. Don't give it any further thought. You have quite enough trouble as it is."

"Oh, I have indeed!" said the dear old lady. "I don't know what I shall do, Mr. King. Philip's death has affected my brother terribly. He was always a quiet man, but now he is so crushed and heart-broken that he is more silent than ever. And I can't seem to comfort him. I think we will have to go away from Maxwell Chimneys. We have a sister out West, and I think we will go out there. I am sure that entire and permanent change of scene is the only thing that will help Alexander at all."

I looked admiringly at the clear lady whose unselfish spirit thought of her brother's comfort, ignoring her own sorrow, and assuring her of my sincere sympathy and my assistance in every possible way, I returned to Hunt.

"I am not surprised," he said, when I told him that Miss Maxwell's clock had undoubtedly been ten minutes slow on Monday evening. "It is alarming, the way the links fit into the chain of evidence, but it must be more than mere coincidence.

"Look at it in this way for a moment—supposing, for the sake of argument, that events proceeded like this:

"You saw Gilbert Crane in the billiard-room at ten o'clock. This you are sure of. Now according to Crane's own statement he looked into Mr. Maxwell's study some twenty minutes later. But we have no other witness for this.

"Mr. Maxwell says he neither heard nor saw him, and Crane himself admits that he did not. With the exception of Miss Gardiner on the balcony, the guests were all in the music-room, not only absorbed in their music, but making a great deal of noise.

"Miss Maxwell was in her own bedroom, and the servants were busy in the kitchens, of which the doors were closed. As nearly as I can find out, Gilbert Crane came running downstairs for Dr. Sheldon a few moments before half past ten. If you have followed my reasoning, you will see that his whereabouts between ten o'clock and, say, ten twenty-five, are unaccounted for except by himself.

"His coat—the automobile coat on which we have discovered the red spots—hung on the hat stand in the back part of the hall. He, therefore, had ample opportunity to leave the billiard-room, put on his coat and the cap and goggles which he always carries in that coat pocket, go up the back staircase, and through the hall window at the head of that staircase out on to the west balcony.

"The library window is directly next to the hall window. He had therefore, I say, both time and opportunity to fire the shots at about ten minutes after ten, which would accord with Miss Maxwell's inaccurate testimony. He had also time and opportunity to return downstairs the way he came, restore his coat to its place on the hat-stand, and go back to the billiard-room.

"This yet left sufficient time for him to go upstairs again—the front stairs this time—in full view of the people in the music-room if they chanced to look, and return to make his startling announcement to Dr. Sheldon."

I had followed Hunt's words with such intense interest that I seemed to be living through the successive scenes myself. As he paused, I remarked thoughtfully:

"And that would explain why Philip cried out, 'Oh, to think that he should shoot me!' "

"Yes," said Hunt gravely, "it explains a great many things. It explains of course the spots on his coat."

"Wait," I cried eagerly, "when the ink spattered on his coat it must also have fallen on his shoes and the bottoms of his trousers."

"Not necessarily on his trousers," said Hunt, "for the coat is long and large, and would probably entirely protect them. As to his shoes, they have doubtless been blackened since, and so all trace would be lost."

"As a chain of circumstantial evidence it is certainly complete," I said, with a sigh. "But all my intuitions cry out against its being the truth."

"Have you any other theory to offer?"

"Not the shadow of one. I only wish I had. But stay. What do you make of Miss Gardiner's assertion that she saw Gilbert placing a pistol in Miss Leslie's hand?"

"I think she is mistaken as to what he was doing. I think Miss Leslie's story is true in every detail. Possibly Mr. Crane endeavored to take the pistol out of her hand, then, changing his mind for some reason, concluded not to do so."

I sat staring at Mr. Hunt, almost stunned by his convincing arguments.

"What will be your next move?" I asked.

"I shall submit this report to Inspector Davis, and he must do whatever he thinks best."

XXI: Circumstantial Evidence

FURTHER investigation only served to strengthen the case against Gilbert Crane.

It was discovered that he owned a thirty-eight caliber pistol. When found, this pistol was properly cleaned and loaded.

It was not rusty, and had every appearance of having been used recently, but how recently who could say?

To my mind the fact that Gilbert possessed a thirty-eight caliber pistol was not a vital bit of evidence. Anybody might possess one. But as Hunt said, it was not contradictory evidence, and, taken in conjunction with the other clues, it was of importance.

It seemed, also, to the authorities, that the motive imputed to Gilbert Crane was a strong one, and among those which most often lead to crime.

And so, Gilbert was arrested and held for trial. Though everybody at Maxwell Chimneys was shocked and astounded at the news of his arrest, it affected them in different ways.

Mildred Leslie was frantic with grief and indignation. She declared that although the intruder might have worn Gilbert's coat, it was positively not Gilbert Crane himself. She vowed she would know Gilbert in any circumstances and in any disguise, and she was sure the man who shot her was a man with whom she was unacquainted, though he was apparently well known to Philip Maxwell.

She grew so excited as to become hysterical, and the doctor ordered that she should again be remanded to absolute seclusion, and allowed to see no one save the nurse and her sister.

Irene Gardiner seemed uncertain as to the justice of the arrest. She viewed the whole matter from a stern, judicial standpoint, and seemed unable to take a personal view of it. I felt sure that she had never liked Mr. Crane, and, feeling equally sure that Mildred was very much in love with him, I could easily understand the different attitudes of the two girls.

I was conscious myself of a growing regard for Irene, and while I could wish her a little softer and more sympathetic toward the prisoner, yet I couldn't help admiring her splendid appreciation of law and justice.

As for the Maxwells, Miss Miranda was so completely crushed already, that another unexpected blow could make but little difference in her demeanor. She said she could not believe Gilbert guilty, but that it was not for her to judge.

Alexander Maxwell showed a like philosophical spirit. After the first shock of surprise, he admitted that justice must have its way, wherever that way might lead; but he again begged us not to be misled by false or incomplete clues, and to prove beyond all doubt whatever we accepted as a fact.

I fully shared the old gentleman's spirit of caution, and kept a vigilant watch on Mr. Hunt's proceedings. But I was forced to admit the evidence all pointed one way, and my only hope lay in the fact that it was purely circumstantial evidence.

Resolved, if possible, to find some weak spot in Hunt's diagnosis of the case, I obtained permission to visit Gilbert Crane in his cell.

I felt a certain embarrassment as I entered, for I expected to see a despairing, broken-down man.

But I found I did not yet know Gilbert Crane. Instead of appearing dejected, he rose to greet me with an expectant look, and held out his hand.

"Will you take it?" he said impulsively, and eagerly. "You need not hesitate. It is the hand of an honest man. I am no more guilty of Philip's death than is Philip himself."

Quite aside from his words, there was honor and truth in the sound of his voice, and the look of his eye. I am very sensitive to deceit, and in every fiber of my being I felt at that moment that an honest man stood before me.

Acting in accordance with this conviction I grasped his hand heartily, and said: "I am sure of it! I admit, and you must admit yourself, that the circumstantial evidence against you is pretty bad. But even before your denial I could not think you guilty, and now you have removed any lurking doubt I may have had."

"Thank you," said Crane simply. "And now I wonder if you can help me."

"It is what I want to do," I said, "but I fear I can do little. I have tried to get at some counter evidence, or refutation of Hunt's theories, but so far I have been unable to do so."

"That's just the point," said Gilbert, in a practical way that seemed to show me a new side of this man. "I don't know myself what to tell you to do. The whole situation is so absurd. To me it is like lightning out of a clear sky. Here am I, arrested for the murder of a man who was one of my best friends. I didn't murder him, and yet circumstances are such that I cannot prove I did not."

"Since we are speaking frankly," I said, "will you tell me if you touched the pistol that Miss Leslie held?"

Gilbert looked at me gravely. "I will," he said. "I ought to have been more straightforward about that, but I didn't mention it, because I thought it of absolutely no importance. When I saw the bodies, I thought that Philip was dead, but that Miss Leslie was still living. I went nearer to look, and on an impulse I started to take the pistol from her hand. But I at once realized that it would be better to call Dr. Sheldon before I touched anything, and I did so."

"You didn't pause to pick up the bronze horse?" I asked.

"Certainly not," was the surprised reply.

"That horse and inkstand play a most mysterious part in the matter. But there must be some explanation for them, and we must find it."

"It will be made clear," said Gilbert, "if you do what I ask."

"I am more than willing to do your bidding," I said.

"Then send for Stone. He is a New York detective, and though I do not know him personally, I know enough about him to feel sure he can unravel this tangle as no one else can."

"How shall I find him?"

"I don't know his address. You will have to go or write to Jack Hemingway; he can tell you. Stone will be expensive, but this is no time for economy. Will you get him?"

"I certainly will," I replied, "and do all in my power to help him."

"Fleming Stone won't need much help," said Gilbert, not ungratefully, but decidedly, "he is a wizard. He can see right through anybody or anything."

"Then he is the man for us, and I'll go for him myself."

"Perhaps," said Crane, after a moment's thought, "it would be wiser not to let it be generally known that he is a celebrated detective."

"All right," I replied; "but the Maxwells will have to know it, because I want to put him up there. They'll be willing, I know. Indeed, Mr. Maxwell has himself suggested that we should get a city detective down."

"I know it," said Gilbert, "but I wish you'd act as if he were just a friend of yours who has a taste for detective work."

"Very well, I'll fix it that way then. But I hate to have you staying here, even for a few days."

"That can't be helped," said Gilbert, "and mustn't be considered. If you can only get Fleming Stone to come down here, I am as good as released."

Glad that he could view the situation in this cheerful manner, I went away, prepared to go at once on Gilbert's errand.

Miss Maxwell hospitably agreed to my proposal to burden her home with another visitor, but Mr. Maxwell did not seem quite pleased.

I couldn't help wondering if he thought that a more astute detective would only succeed in proving Gilbert's guilt more conclusively. He expressed himself as thinking it wise to let well enough alone, but as he made no definite protest against my going, I went to New York that very day in search of Fleming Stone. I found him, and after some persuasion, I induced him to return to Hamilton with me in the interests of Gilbert Crane.

Never shall I forget the delight of my first long conversation with Fleming Stone.

As to personal appearance, he was a fine-looking man without being in any way remarkably handsome. He was large and well-formed, between forty and fifty years old, with iron-gray hair and a clear, healthy complexion. His eyes were his chief charm and their attraction lay largely in their expression, and in their surrounding dark lashes and brows. Mr. Stone had a kindly smile, and his face in repose seemed to denote an even temper and a gracious disposition. He was possessed of great personal magnetism, and the liking which I felt for him the first moment I saw him, grew rapidly into admiration.

On the way down, at his request, I told him everything I knew about the Maxwell mystery. He was intensely interested; and I was secretly filled with joy when he expressed a decided approval of the methods I had used in discovering the red ink.

After I had told him every detail of the story, he changed the subject courteously, but very decidedly, and talked of other matters. He was a brilliant conversationalist, which surprised me, for my mental picture of a great detective had always represented a most taciturn gentleman of sinister aspect.

When we reached Maxwell Chimneys it was nearly dinner time.

At the dinner table, Mr. Stone gave no hint of his profession either in manner or appearance. He was simply a well-bred, well-dressed gentleman, with irreproachable manners and a talent for interesting conversation.

I noticed that Mr. Maxwell looked at him with occasional furtive glances, and seemed to be mentally weighing the man's professional ability. Either he was satisfied with the result of his scrutiny, or the charm of Mr. Stone appealed to him, for he distinctly showed a liking for his new guest before the close of the meal.

As Mildred Leslie was not yet allowed to leave her room, the Whitings and Miss Gardiner made up the rest of the dinner guests.

Edith Whiting and her husband were always to be depended on for a correct demeanor of any sort that the situation might require, but I was anxious to see what attitude Irene would assume toward the newcomer.

To my surprise she showed an intense interest in him.

She seemed fairly eager lest she lose one word of his conversation, and her brilliant cheeks and shining eyes proved her vivid enjoyment of the occasion.

After dinner there was music. In addition to his other talents, Mr. Stone was a musician, and though he declined to play for us that night, he seemed thoroughly to enjoy the music we made for him.

Though quite content to leave matters in his hands, I couldn't help wondering when he intended to begin his detective work. But almost as if in answer to my thought, Mr. Stone remarked that if it met with the approval of them all, he would ask for a short but absolutely private interview with each one.

"I assume there are no secrets among us," he said, in his winning way, "and as I understand the situation, from what Mr. King has told me, I think we are all earnestly anxious to discover the person who took the life of Philip Maxwell."

This was said gravely, almost solemnly, and for a moment no one spoke. Then Miss Maxwell said, in her gentle voice, "I trust I am not too revengeful in spirit, but I own I would be glad to see the slayer of my boy brought to justice."

Fleming Stone seemed to consider this an authority to proceed in his own way. Asking Miss Maxwell to go with him to the study, he escorted her from the room with an air of courtly grace that sat well upon him.

After not more than ten minutes, Mr. Stone brought her back, and asked that he might next have a few words with Mr. Maxwell. When the two men had gone, Miss Maxwell gave voice to her admiration of her new guest and declared that she had never seen anyone who gave her such favorable first impressions. We all agreed with her, and were enthusiastic in our praise of Fleming Stone as a man, whatever he might prove to be as a detective.

When Mr. Maxwell's short interview was finished, the others were taken in turn, and I was somewhat surprised to notice that Mr. Stone detained Tom Whiting far longer than any of the rest.

When he finally rejoined the group in the music room, Fleming Stone said:

"These preliminary and perhaps not entirely necessary formalities are now over; and I think I have learned all that I need to know from you who are here. I can, of course, do nothing more tonight. Tomorrow I must ask for a short talk with Miss Leslie, and after that I will see Mr. Crane."

But later that evening, Fleming Stone and I had a short conference in the library. I showed him the horse and the inkstand; described the exact position of Philip and Mildred when they were found; showed him where the black spangles were discovered; and pointed out how the balcony floor had been marked by signs of an apparent scuffle. Mr. Stone showed an unexpected interest in this last-named clue, though I confess it had seemed to me the least important of any. The balcony had since been swept, but there were still visible slight scratches in the long, sweeping marks I have described.

"I do not deduce from these scratches that there was a scuffle," said Mr. Stone. "That is, not in the sense of there having been a struggle between two persons. I see no reason for thinking that these marks were made by more than one pair of feet."

"Mr. Stone," I said, almost timidly, "perhaps I have no right to ask, but have your suspicions fallen in any direction as yet?"

Fleming Stone looked at me with an expression of sorrow in his deep gray eyes.

"I will tell you," he said, "for I know you will not betray my confidence, that I am positively certain who the criminal is; that it is not Gilbert Crane; and that it is a person upon whom I can lay my hand at any moment."

XXII: Fleming Stone's Discoveries

THE next morning, although Fleming Stone was the same affable, courteous gentleman that he had been the night before, yet there was a shade more of seriousness in his manner. He spoke cheerfully, but it seemed to be with an effort, and I felt a vague sense of an impending disaster which might be worse than anything that had gone before.

After breakfast, Mr. Hunt came over and in the fateful library he was introduced to Fleming Stone. I was present at their interview, and I was glad to see that the two men at once assumed cordial attitudes, and seemed prepared to work together harmoniously.

I think Hunt may have felt a natural professional jealousy of the city detective, but if so he showed no trace of it. Besides, Mr. Hunt was quite at the end of his resources—completely baffled by the case. If Gilbert Crane were not the guilty man, neither our local detective nor myself knew where to look for the criminal.

Our discussion in the library did not last long, but it was exceedingly business-like and to the point. Without losing a shade of his graceful politeness, Fleming Stone showed also the quick working of his direct, forceful mind. He approved of all that Hunt and I had done. In a few words he commended our methods and accepted our results.

Then in silence he scrutinized the library. I think nothing in the room escaped the swift, thorough glances of those dark eyes. He rose to examine the rug, and the window casing, and then stepped out on the balcony to look at the scratches of which I had told him. These latter were very faint, but with a large magnifying glass which he took from his pocket he examined them carefully and seemed satisfied with what he found.

Returning to the library, he took the waste paper basket from under the desk and examined its contents. It was empty save for a few scraps of torn paper which I had thrown there myself the day before, but I saw his action with a sudden shock of dismay.

Neither Hunt nor I had thought of looking in the waste-basket, and though I had no definite hope of anything to be found there, it was a chance we ought not to have lost.

"Did Mr. Philip Maxwell ever write letters in this room?" asked Mr. Stone.

"Sometimes he did," I replied, "but more often he wrote down in his uncle's study."

"But he might have opened letters and read them here?"

"Yes; he used this desk a great deal."

"Where are the papers from the waste-baskets thrown?"

"I don't know, Mr. Stone; but the servants can tell you. Shall I call the maid who attends to the cleaning of this room?"

"I wish you would do so; then we will consider this consultation at an end. I have no wish to be unduly secret about my plans, but I must work uninterruptedly today, for I think developments will come thick and fast."

Mr. Hunt and I left the library, and I at once sent the maid to Mr. Stone as he had requested. Less than fifteen minutes later, I saw him coming up from the cellar. Seeing that I was alone, he said: "I found a paper that is a most important link in our chain. Will you look at it a moment?"

He drew from his pocket a paper which had evidently been smoothed out after being much crumpled, and turned down the top of the sheet so that I did not see the address. "That is Mr. Philip Maxwell's handwriting, is it not?" he said.

"Yes," I replied, and in Phil's well-known characters I read:

At last I have discovered the truth, and it has broken my heart. Even now I could not believe it, but your...

The writing stopped abruptly, and the letter had evidently been thrown aside unfinished. I restrained my intense curiosity, and did not ask to see the name at the head of the letter, but apparently Fleming Stone divined my thoughts.

"You will know only too soon," he said with that sad note in his voice that always thrilled me. "Now I am going to see Miss Leslie."

The doctor had permitted a short interview, and I learned afterward from Edith Whiting, that though Mildred had dreaded it, she was at once put at her ease by Mr. Stone's gentleness, and gave a brief but coherent account of the affair.

It was shortly before noon that I went for a walk with Irene Gardiner. As we went away, I saw Mr. Stone and Miss Miranda Maxwell in the music room. Miss Maxwell was knitting some fleecy white-wool thing, and though she looked sad she was calm and unexcited.

They seemed to be chatting cozily, and yet I felt sure that Fleming Stone was learning some details about Philip's life or character which he considered important.

I sighed to think that the net was certainly closing in around somebody, and the amazing part was that I had not the remotest idea toward whom Fleming Stone's suspicions were directed. Miss Gardiner and I walked down the path to the river. As was inevitable, we talked only of the all-absorbing topic, and especially of Fleming Stone.

"Isn't he wonderful?" she exclaimed.

"He is certainly the ideal detective."

"He is in his methods and his intellect," I said, "but his personal appearance is far from my preconceived notions of the regulation detective. I had always imagined them grim and sinister. This man is not only affable but positively sunny."

"He is fascinating!" declared Irene. "I have never met anyone who seemed so attractive at first sight."

I quite agreed with her, but I was suddenly conscious of an absurd pang of jealousy. I was beginning to think that Irene Gardiner was pretty nearly necessary to the happiness of my life, and this avowed interest of hers in another man spurred me to a sudden conclusion that I cared for her very much indeed. But this was no time or place to tell her so. At the Maxwells' invitation she had decided to remain at Maxwell Chimneys with the Whitings until Mildred was able to travel to New York. Dr. Sheldon had said that the journey might safely be taken about the middle of the following week. I had made my plans to go at the same time, but in view of the rapid developments of the past two days I had unmade those plans and had made no others.

"Doesn't it seem strange," said Irene, "that you and I were talking about crime and criminals on the way down here last week? How little we thought that we were coming straight to a tragedy."

"It is a tragedy," I said, "and it may prove even more of a one than we yet know. Irene, if Gilbert didn't shoot Philip, have you any idea who did?"

"No," she said, looking at me with a candor in her eyes which left no room for doubt.

"No, I have not the faintest idea. And yet I cannot believe Gilbert did it. I never liked him, but he does not seem to me capable of crime."

"And yet you hold the theory that, given an opportunity, we are all capable of crime."

"I know I said that," said Irene thoughtfully.

"And it does seem true in theory, but it is hard to believe it in an individual case."

"I am sure Gilbert was not the criminal," I said, "but my certainty is based on something quite apart from the question of his capability in the way of committing crime. First, I was convinced of his innocence by his own attitude. A simple assertion might be false, but Gilbert's look and voice and manner told far more than his words. No criminal could have acted as he did. Even his scornful indifference to the fact of his arrest carried conviction of his innocence. But aside from all that, Fleming Stone says he knows that Gilbert is not guilty, and moreover he knows who is."

"He knows who is!" exclaimed Irene. "Who can it be?"

"I don't know; but I am sure from what Mr. Stone says it is someone whom we all know, and whose conviction will not only surprise but sadden us."

"Do you suppose," said Irene slowly, her great eyes wide with horror, "that it could have been Mildred after all?"

So this strange girl had dared to put into words a thought which I had tried hard to keep out of my mind.

"Don't!" said I, "I cannot think of it!"

"But her whole story about the intruder may have been a fabrication."

"Don't," I said again, "such remarks are unworthy of you—are unworthy of any woman."

"You always misunderstand me," said Irene impatiently.

"I do?"

"I don't mean it the way you think. If I could see Mildred myself, I would talk to her in the same way. There is no harm in asking a frank question."

"Then," I said abruptly. "I will ask you one. What did you mean last Monday night when you told me that if I wouldn't interfere between Philip and Mildred you would take matters into your own hands?"

"I am not at all offended by your question," said Irene, looking me straight in the eyes, "neither do I assume that, because you ask it, you think that I meant anything desperate. I meant only what I said—that if you wouldn't advise Philip Maxwell not to be infatuated by such a foolish, artful little coquette as Mildred Leslie, then I would warn him myself."

"Since we are speaking frankly, I must admit that it would seem to me unwarranted interference on your part."

"I suppose I am peculiar," said Irene with a sigh, "but it doesn't seem that way to me. However, this is a question capable of much discussion. Suppose we leave its consideration for some other time, and return to the house now."

We walked back, chatting in a lighter vein, and somehow my heart sank when I saw Fleming Stone sitting alone on the veranda. It may have been imagination, or perhaps intuition, but as soon as I saw him, I felt a conviction that he had accomplished his work, and that we would soon know the result.

"I've been waiting for you," he said, as I went toward him.

Irene went into the house, and Mr. Stone continued.

"I have discovered everything, and I want you to be prepared for a sad revelation."

"Did you learn anything from your interview with Miss Leslie?" I asked impulsively.

"Nothing more than I knew before I saw her," he replied, and his inscrutable face gave me no glimmer of information.

"It is almost one o'clock," he went on, "and after luncheon I will tell you all. I have asked Mr. Hunt to be present, and you will both please meet me in the library at two o'clock."

Somehow the sad foreboding that had taken possession of me made me glad of even an hour's further respite. I went to the luncheon table and made my bravest endeavor to seem my natural self. But a depressing cloud seemed to hang over us all. Although each one tried to be cheerful, the efforts were far from being entirely successful.

Even Mr. Maxwell seemed disturbed. Indeed, Miss Miranda was most placid of all, and I felt sure that was due to the calming effect of Mr. Stone's kindly consideration for her. At last the meal was over, and, unable to keep up the strain any longer I went at once to the library, and awaited the others.

Mr. Hunt came first. "Have you any idea of the disclosure Mr. Stone is about to make?" he said to me.

"No," said I, "I think I can truthfully say I haven't."

"He has asked Dr. Sheldon to be here by half past two," said Hunt.

Again my thoughts flew to Mildred Leslie, but I said nothing.

Then Fleming Stone came into the room. There was sadness still in his eyes, but he had again assumed that alert, official air which characterized his professional moments.

"Gentlemen," he said, "I came down here, as you know, an absolute stranger and entirely unprejudiced. I have listened to various accounts of the crime; I have weighed the evidence offered to me; I have made investigations on my own account and drawn my own deductions.

"I have considered the character and dispositions of all persons known to be in the vicinity of Philip Maxwell at the time of his death; have pondered over the possible motive for the crime; and, from the facts learned as a result of my investigation and consideration, I have discovered the murderer.

"Gentlemen, Philip Maxwell was shot by his uncle, Mr. Alexander Maxwell!"

XXIII: The Confession

THERE was nothing to be said.

I was silent, because I felt as if the earth had suddenly given way beneath me, and all was chaos. Not for a moment did I doubt Fleming Stone's statement, for his words compelled conviction.

But in the confused mass of sudden thoughts that surged through my brain, I seemed to see clearly nothing but Miss Miranda's placid face, and I cried out involuntarily:

"Don't let his sister know!"

Hunt sat like a man stunned. His expression was positively vacant, and I think he was trying to realize what Mr. Stone's announcement meant.

"It is terrible, I know," said Fleming Stone, "and I quite appreciate the shock it must be to you. But inexorable justice demands that we proceed without faltering. I think that, without telling you of the various steps which led me to this conclusion, I can best prove to you that it is the true one by asking you to go with me while I lay the facts before Mr. Maxwell. I think his reception of what I have to say, and the visible effect of my accusations upon him, will prove to you beyond any possible doubt his connection with the crime. Indeed, from what I know of the man I am disposed to think he will make full confession of his guilt."

Fleming Stone's words sounded to me like a voice heard in a dream; and even my own voice sounded strange and unreal, as I murmured: "It will kill him. He has heart disease."

"I know it," said Fleming Stone, "and I, too, fear the effect upon him. For that reason I have asked Dr. Sheldon to be present."

When Dr. Sheldon arrived, he came directly to us in the library, and Fleming Stone told him in a few words of the ordeal we had to undergo.

The four of us then went down to Mr. Maxwell's study. We found him there alone. We all went in, and Fleming Stone closed the door. He stood for a moment looking directly at Mr. Maxwell, and his deep eyes were filled with a great compassion.

"Mr. Maxwell," he said—and his voice though quiet was most impressive—"we have come to tell you that we have discovered that Philip Maxwell died by your hand."

If any of us had doubted Alexander Maxwell's guilt—and I think some of us had—all possibility of doubt was at once removed.

If ever I saw a face on which confession was stamped as plainly as on a printed page, it was Alexander Maxwell's face at that moment. Instinctively, I turned away, but almost immediately I heard Mr. Maxwell gasp, and I knew that Fleming Stone's expectations had been verified, and that Mr. Maxwell's heart had not been able to stand the shock.

Dr. Sheldon sprang to his side, and with the assistance of the others laid the unconscious man on the couch.

"He is not dead," said Dr. Sheldon, after a few moments. "And he will soon rally from this; but I feel sure it is a fatal attack. I think he cannot live more than a few hours."

As the doctor had surmised, Mr. Maxwell soon rallied and spoke:

"Don't let Miranda know," he said, "don't ever let Miranda know."

Fleming Stone stepped forward.

"Mr. Maxwell," he said, "if you will make a full confession in the presence of these gentlemen, I will promise you on my honor that I will use every endeavor to keep the knowledge of your guilt from your sister."

"I will not only assist Mr. Stone in his endeavor," said Dr. Sheldon, "but I think I can safely promise that Miss Miranda shall never learn the secret. You are very ill, Mr. Maxwell, and whatever you wish to say must be said at once."

"I am ready," said Alexander Maxwell, and though his voice was faint, and though he seemed to realize his own fearful position, yet his manner expressed a certainly sense of relief which I believed to be due to the relaxation of the tension of fear he had been under so long.

"I am ready," he said again, "and, to make clear to you the motive for my deed, I must begin my story many years back."

"But you must make it brief," said Dr. Sheldon. "I cannot allow you to talk long at this time."

"There will not be any other time," said Mr. Maxwell quietly.

I could not help marveling at this strange man, whose wonderful power of self-control did not desert him in this moment of mental and physical extremity.

Mr. Maxwell proceeded, and Fleming Stone took stenographic notes of his statement.

"Twenty-five years ago I lived in California and so did my brother John. Though not partners, our business interests were closely united in many ways. My brother married, and, about a year after Philip's birth, his wife died.

"Five years later, John Maxwell died, and left the whole of his large fortune with me in trust for Philip. Although it was supposed at that time that my own fortune was as large or larger than John's, the reverse was true.

I had lost much money in unfortunate speculation, and it was to my surprise that I discovered the large amount of money my brother had left behind him.

"I used this money to make good my losses, trusting to replace it with further gains of my own before Philip should come of age. I was always a close-mouthed man, and neither Miranda nor my other sister, Hannah, knew anything about John's money.

"I came East to live, and after some years the lawyer who was the only one beside myself who knew the circumstances died. Having by this time become a well-known and respected citizen of Hamilton, being president of the bank, and holding, or having held, various public offices, my pride and ambition rebelled at giving up my entire fortune to Philip.

"But it would have taken all my available assets to make up the sum entrusted to me by the boy's father. For many years I struggled with this temptation, and at last, when Philip was twenty one, I succumbed.

"On his twenty-first birthday, instead of telling him the truth, I offered him a permanent home at Maxwell Chimneys and agreed to support him indulgently and even extravagantly."

Here, at the very climax of the recital, Mr. Maxwell sank back upon the couch, breathless and exhausted. But after a moment's rest he continued:

"We lived happily enough for a few years—in fact, until one day about a fortnight ago.

"That morning I was here in my study and had spread out before me the principal papers relating to the trust I had held for Philip.

"Suddenly I was called to the telephone and, thinking to return in a minute, left the papers on my desk. But I was detained at the telephone much longer than I anticipated, and, when I returned, although there was nobody in sight, it seemed to me the papers had been disturbed.

"They were tossed about, and I felt a presentiment that Philip had been in there and had read them. It would have been no breach of honor on his part, for he had always been allowed free access to my study and to my business papers.

"From that time on Philip was a changed man. His manner toward me confirmed my suspicion that he had discovered my guilt. No mention was made of the subject between us, but for more than a week Philip continued to act like a man crushed by a sudden disaster.

"Last Monday he wrote a letter to me in which he told me that he had discovered the truth, and that he felt he was entitled to an explanation. This explanation I knew I could not give, nor was I willing to face my nephew's well-deserved condemnation and the exposure of my treachery to the public.

"On Monday then, after reading Philip's letter, I determined that I would take my own life, as being a cowardly but final solution of my difficulties.

"Monday evening I sat in my study and decided that the time had come. I had placed my pistol in my pocket, and had intended to go up to my own room and there expiate my guilt toward my brother and his son.

"At this moment, Mr. King chanced to come into my study, and mentioned that Philip and Mildred were in the library. This strengthened my purpose, for I felt sure that Philip was even then telling Miss Leslie that he was in reality a rich man.

"Mr. King went on through the billiard-room and across the hall to the music-room. I left the study at once, and saw Mr. King enter the music room door.

"As I crossed the back part of the hall, I felt an impulse to look once more on Philip's face. I knew I could step out on the balcony from the hall window and look in at the library window unobserved.

"It has always been my habit when going out for a moment into the night air to catch up any coat from the hat-stand and throw it around me. I did this mechanically, and it chanced to be Gilbert Crane's automobile coat.

"I went up the back stairs, putting the coat on as I went. Instinctively putting my hands into the pockets, I felt there the cap and goggles.

"It was then that the evil impulse seized me. I saw my beautiful home with its rich appointments, its lights, and its flowers; I heard the gay music and laughter; and like a flash it came to me that Philip should be the one to give up all that, and not I.

"I realized, as by an inspiration, that the goggles and a turned-up coat-collar would be ample disguise, and I thought the crime would be attributed to an outside marauder.

"The rest you know. Philip recognized me. But Miss Leslie did not. That is all."

Mr. Maxwell fell back, and Dr. Sheldon, thinking the end had come, went toward him.

But Fleming Stone, the inexorable, leaned forward, and said distinctly to Mr. Maxwell: "Wait—did you refill the inkstand?"

"Yes," said Mr. Maxwell, with a sudden revival of strength, "yes. I returned to the room late that night, picked up the inkstand, washed it, refilled it, and replaced it. The bronze horse I picked up and replaced before leaving the room the first time."

I gazed at Alexander Maxwell, wonderingly. And yet, for a man who could live the life he had lived, who could conduct himself as he had during the past week, it was not strange that he was able thus, in the face of death, calmly to relate these details of his own crime.

"One more thing," said Mr. Stone. "Did you scrape your foot around on the balcony to efface a possible footprint?"

"Yes; I knew the dust was thick there, and I wished to eliminate all traces."

Here Mr. Maxwell's strength seemed to leave him all at once. On the verge of total collapse, he said again, "Don't let Miranda know "—and then sank into unconsciousness.

"He will probably not rally again," said Dr. Sheldon. "I think his sister should be notified at once of his illness. But we shall all agree that she must not know of his crime."

"Shall I call her?" I volunteered, as no one else moved to do so.

"Yes," said Dr. Sheldon.

"She will be startled, but it will not be entirely unexpected. I have warned her for years that the end would come like this."

In justice to the innocent, Fleming Stone and I went at once to Inspector Davis to ask that Gilbert Crane be released. The order for release was sent immediately, and at last we were free to ask Fleming Stone a few questions.

"How did you do it?" cried Hunt, in his abrupt way.

"How did you do it so soon?" cried I, no less curious.

"It was not difficult," said Fleming Stone, in that direct way of his, which was not over-modest, but simply truthful.

"Mr. King's statement, which was the first one I heard, showed me that, although Mr. Crane's alibi from ten o'clock till half past ten depended entirely upon his own uncorroborated word, yet Mr. Maxwell's alibi was equally without verification.

"Mr. King saw Mr. Maxwell in his study at ten o'clock. He was found there again sometime after ten-thirty. This proved nothing but the opportunity. Then all the evidence regarding the coat, the clues found in the library, and elsewhere, would apply to him as well as to Crane. It remained, however, to find what motive, if any, could have impelled Alexander Maxwell to the deed.

"I had not talked with him ten minutes before I concluded that he was a man with a secret. Miss Maxwell supplied a clue when she told me what she knew of Philip's early history.

"Another clue was the crumpled letter found among the waste paper. This was addressed to Alexander Maxwell, and was probably begun and discarded for the one which Philip wrote and sent to his uncle.

"The fact that the inkstand had been refilled and replaced argued someone familiar with the library; even Gilbert Crane would not be apt to know where the supply of red ink was kept. Everything pointed in one direction.

"But perhaps the most convincing clue was given to me last evening by Mr. Maxwell himself. You remember, Mr. King, that I took each member of the household to the study separately. When I interviewed Mr. Maxwell there, I took care not to alarm him, but rather to put him at his ease as much as possible.

"Noticing a well-worn foot-rest, I felt sure that it was his habit to sit with his feet up on it. In hopes of his taking this position, I asked him to show me just how he was sitting when the news of the crime was brought to him.

"As I surmised, he sat down in his big armchair, and put his feet upon the footrest. This gave me an opportunity to examine the soles of his shoes, and I discovered on one of them a large stain of a dull, purplish red. The stain made by red ink is indelible and of a peculiar tinge, so that I felt sure this was the man at whom the inkstand had been thrown, and who had unknowingly stepped upon a wet spot of red ink.

"Owing to the awkward goggles which he wore, and, too, the excitement of the moment, he probably did not notice the ink at all. When he returned later, the spots had sunk into the crimson rug, and partly dried. The shoes were light house-shoes, and probably he did not wear them out of doors, for dampness or hard wear would have tended to obliterate the stain.

"As it was, the color could plainly be seen. I am sure that a chemical test would prove it to be a stain of red ink."

Mr. Maxwell died that night, and Dr. Sheldon at once took Miss Miranda to his own home, and kept her there, safely out of the reach of gossip until she went out to Colorado to live with her sister. Her nerves were shattered, and she begged so piteously that she might not be obliged to enter Maxwell Chimneys again, that her wishes were willingly respected. The rest of us remained at the house until the sister, Hannah, came to take charge of affairs, and to take Miss Miranda home with her.

"It is a case," I said to Irene Gardiner, "which proves your theory—the murder of Philip Maxwell was brought about solely by opportunity.

"My chance remark to Mr. Maxwell that the young people were in the library; the inadvertent snatching up of Gilbert's coat; the fact that the goggles and cap were in the pocket; the fact that Philip's uncle had a weapon with him—all these things form tiny links in a strong chain of opportunity."

"But the evil impulse must have been in his heart, or he would never have taken advantage of this opportunity," said Irene, unconsciously refuting a theory she had herself advanced.

"I would rather not think," said Fleming Stone, in his sweet, serious voice, "that opportunity creates a sinner, or even that it creates an evil impulse. I would rather believe—and I do believe—that opportunity only warms into action an evil impulse that is lying dormant; and I do not believe that dormant evil impulse is in everybody."

"Nor do I," said Irene; "it would be a sad world, indeed, if that were true. And yet," she looked at me, "I confess I used to think so. But I have learned much in the last few weeks, and I realize how difficult it is to judge what anyone would do or would not do upon occasion. And yet I would rather believe that the evil impulse was created in Mr. Maxwell's mind by the especial opportunity, than to think he had all his life been a man capable of crime."

"Perhaps you're right," said Stone; "and after all, it makes little difference. The thing is to have a strong enough character or will to resist any evil impulse or any special opportunity that may present itself. And that no one can declare he possesses, until he has been tried and proven. But let us be thankful that the opportunities are comparatively rare and the natures that succumb to them are rarer still."

"It is a satisfaction to realize that," I returned, "but that very knowledge makes it seem all the more strange and sad that an exceptional case should be this of Alexander Maxwell."

THE END

Made in the USA
Monee, IL
24 June 2022